INSIDE OUT

 LITTLE, BROWN AND COMPANY
Boston   Toronto   London

INSIDE
OUT

A Musical Adventure

ELIZABETH SWADOS

First edition

Library of Congress Cataloging-in-Publication Data
Swados, Elizabeth.
Inside out : a musical adventure / Elizabeth Swados.
    p. cm.
Summary: Two indifferent music students find themselves
in a world made up of musical instruments who need their
help to fight against the evil Duke of Sharps and Queen of
Flat Notes and their plan to eliminate all music.
ISBN 0-316-82466-6
[1. Musical instruments—Fiction. 2. Fantasy.] I. Title.
PZ7.S969878In 1989 [Fic]—dc19   89-31327 CIP AC

10 9 8 7 6 5 4 3 2 1

BP

Published simultaneously in Canada
by Little, Brown & Company (Canada) Limited
Printed in the United States of America

To the memory of Jerry Lurie

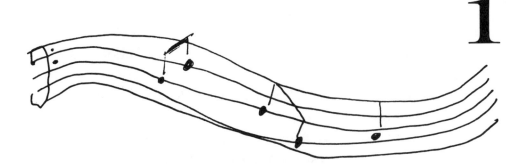

The Bad Music Lesson

THERE IS NOTHING worse than having to take a music lesson when you don't want to. It's much the same as having to eat your peas mashed into your potatoes or having your neck scrubbed with a rough washcloth early in the morning.

Unwanted music lessons often sound very bad. A drum lesson can sound as if a blind cat got lost in the kitchen. A violin lesson can sound like fingernails being scraped across the blackboard. A really bad lesson sounds as if someone's stepping on an already stubbed toe. But a bad piano lesson can be just plain boring. It's more boring than Aunt Theresa's slides of old pillars and broken-down statues from her trip to Europe, more boring than Uncle Wilber's lightbulb jokes.

Gemma and George were twins and, except for one being a boy and the other a girl, they looked nearly exactly alike. They were nine years old and had bright red hair, which is a fabulous and magical thing. When you have red hair it's as if you have a bright flame attached to you, and people give you presents when you least expect them to.

George and Gemma's mother was a very famous and wonderful flute player, and she insisted that the twins take music lessons twice a week. She said music lessons would "open all kinds of doors for them."

The twins loved their mother more than anyone else but didn't love music lessons at all. You see, even though the twins were kindhearted and smart, they had a good deal of difficulty sitting still. They were a bit spoiled and didn't like listening to their music teacher's rules. The twins preferred to play with their instruments as if they were fighting with each other in the playroom, and this was fun but very disrespectful. Gemma liked to try to stab George with her violin bow, while George tried to

glue Gemma's fingers onto the piano keys. Gemma often tried to hang her small violin on George's nose by its strings, while George tried to squash Gemma under the piano lid. They had been terrible students for a whole year, and never ceased coming up with ways to be naughty.

Every Tuesday and Thursday their mother prayed to God and dropped the twins at the Harmony Center Music School. The school was located in the back room of an old musical instrument store. The store was located in an old Victorian mansion full of curving hallways, steep stairways, and odd little doors. Instruments lay out in antique velvet display cases and seemed much too precious to touch. The old peeling walls and curling wooden cases were filled with shining violins, violas, cellos. The cases had harmonicas, kazoos, finger cymbals, ocarinas, bongos, silver flutes, clarinets, oboes, and instruments from countries so far away the twins didn't know their names. It was all very spooky. The twins had to walk past the display cases through the big ballroom with its arched cathedral ceiling and shadowy wall. In that room there stood the large majestic instruments like the basses and timpani, the harps, gongs, and contrabassoons. The instruments looked like serious people having a very serious conference. It was known that this old music store was owned by the one and only Mr. VagenWorgenVurst, a great musician and formidable teacher. He gave his lessons at the end of the great room located way at the back of the store. His grand piano, desks, couches, instruments, and blackboards were set up right in the store so he could hear customers in case they came in while he was teaching. To Gemma and George their lesson was like spending an hour in a great haunted house full of odd shadows and looming figures.

Mr. Phineas VagenWorgenVurst didn't help. He was suppos-

edly the greatest music teacher for miles around, but he was timid and a little strange. He was small, shaped like a pear, and had a gray-and-white-striped goatee. He had beady eyes like a bat. He wore tap shoes. He laughed through his nose in little squeaks. He breathed through his mouth, and when he breathed in he sounded like a vacuum cleaner. When he breathed out it looked dusty and moths flew from his mouth. He owned a tiny Pekinese dog named Kafka.

He was very strange. He often disappeared behind his great velvet curtains, counting "Vun too tree four! Vun too tree four!" the whole time. He was undoubtedly strange. Sometimes he held a white baton and tapped Gemma's wrist with it, or poked

George on the nose. Sometimes Mr. VagenWorgenVurst just scratched his own ear with the baton and shook his head. He whinnied like a horse, and a pigeon flew out of his nose. He was indeed strange.

Mr. VagenWorgenVurst had other very peculiar ways. When either Gemma or George played wrong notes, his cheeks puffed out and he turned a purplish brownish color. His ears seemed to grow. The pigeons, frogs, salamanders, and hummingbirds he carried in his back and side pockets began to stare out from his pants and then hopped and gurgled and squeaked. He sometimes lit candles and threw darts at black balloons filled with powder. If Gemma and George had not practiced their assignments (which they rarely did), Mr. VagenWorgenVurst threw himself onto the velvet chaise longue near his velvet purple draperies and burst into pitiful sobs. When he sobbed, Kafka began to bark in yips so high and sharp they hurt Gemma and George's fillings.

"Oh, you've killed them," sobbed Mr. VagenWorgenVurst. "You've slaughtered my precious notes. You insensitive children. Ones like you should be sent to musician's prison for cruel and unusual harmonies."

It was hard for Gemma and George to concentrate, for every time Mr. VagenWorgenVurst lay on his stomach, sobbing on his chaise longue, they could see a pigeon or a frog staring out from the back pocket of his pants. Usually Gemma was the first to start to laugh and George would follow. They went from a low chortle to a loud chuckle to an all-out Hee-Haw.

Music lessons often ended with Mr. VagenWorgenVurst's unhappy weeping, his dog barking, and his other pets bobbing out from his pockets.

"How can you hurt my notes that way?" Mr. Vagen-WorgenVurst hiccupped. His voice followed the twins as they bolted into the afternoon air, relieved to have gotten over one more hour, ready now to play softball or badminton, or to cook a mud-and-peanut-brittle pudding with a dash of Dad's Old Spice after-shave.

One particular terrible Thursday (it was a Thursday in July because summer was the *worst* time for music lessons), Gemma had not even bothered to read her violin assignment from the Tuesday before, and George had folded up his music paper in order to construct an origami-style Boeing Concorde jet.

"What'll we tell Mr. VagenWorgenVurst?" George whispered to Gemma in their mother's car. "We have nothing to play for him."

Gemma was watching the sun on the leaves. Summer was her favorite season. She was too lazy to care.

They tiptoed through the music store pretending to be very brave indeed. On this particular terrible day, however, when they'd been even *more* lazy than before, the aisles in the music store seemed thin and treacherous. They kept changing size and creaking as if to try to squeeze Gemma and George like an amusement-park laughing-house game. The big bass fiddles, harps, and gongs loomed from the walls, and their shadows took on the shapes of gnomes, gargoyles, and dragons.

When the lesson began, Mr. VagenWorgenVurst looked scarier than ever. His eyebrows knit together. He wore glasses like fishbowls and a suit whose sleeves were too short. He had a yellow slip of paper clipped to his beard. It said "Remember to call the plumber."

George sat at the piano and Gemma reluctantly unpacked her violin.

"Well, my little sveeties," Mr. VagenWorgenVurst said. He had an accent that whistled on its *s*'s, stuttered on its *t*'s and made *w*'s sound like *v*'s. Therefore "sweeties" came out "soo-veet't'iesooo." He rubbed his hands together and they made a sandpapery sound.

"Play away," said Mr. VagenWorgenVurst.

Gemma and George started to play, and what came out were the worst sounds in the history of the whole world. The music was so sour that the wood walls of Mr. VagenWorgenVurst's studio curled in. The lightbulbs dimmed. Animals up and down the block yowled, and it began to rain. Mr. VagenWorgenVurst's glasses fogged up.

"Oh, my," he whispered. "Oh, my." His old, knotty hands went into fists and he began to stamp his feet up and down as if playing a furious game of hopscotch.

"There ought to be a law," he shouted. "Some kind of ordinance against children who pulverize music."

Gemma and George continued to play because, although they sounded just dreadful, they were having a good time. Gemma plunked at the piano with her violin bow, and George screeched an imitation of its high, squeaky notes. Both yelled, laughed, and pulled at each other's hair, while Mr. VagenWorgenVurst chased after them, gathering his poor music tenderly to his chest.

Then Mr. VagenWorgenVurst began to jump straight up and down as if on a pogo stick. Suddenly his music pages lit up. "What's this?" he called out. The notes left the page and flew around the room in a magical circle. The notes chanted and throbbed. "Look what you've done!" cried the music teacher as the notes exploded into a show of fireworks.

The notes made a formidable mountain and leaned over him. "They're angry!" he cried. "Now you've got some explaining to do!" Mr. VagenWorgenVurst knelt and toddled on his knees. Then he began to crawl.

"There ought to be an inoculation against children playing music," he screamed. "You should be allowed only your clay and dolls." Meanwhile the notes slapped against the walls like bats and the lights went on and off.

With the lights blinking, the animals leaping, flying, and howling, the rain hissing, and the walls curling, it seemed the commotion couldn't get any worse, but something else happened. Mr. VagenWorgenVurst began to sneeze. And, for a little old man with a goatee, he let out a huge sneeze. It was like a great wind. The music paper circled up and flew out the window. Mr. VagenWorgenVurst sneezed again and the lights swayed, pillows flew off the chaise longue, and the bow in Gemma's hair came undone.

"Please stop that," Gemma said sternly. (She was the less patient of the twins.)

"I can't," moaned Mr. VagenWorgenVurst. "This whole thing has aggravated my allergy." It was true. He'd swelled to the shape of a tomato. "I'm allergic to horrible music."

Mr. VagenWorgenVurst sneezed again, and this time it was as strong and turbulent as a tornado.

"We'd better hold on to something," George (the more practical of the twins) shouted. At first there seemed to be nothing to hold on to. Papers, pets, and pillows swirled around like a fast-moving Ferris wheel. Gemma and George began to be frightened.

"Stop sneezing, Mr. VagenWorgenVurst," Gemma shouted, "and we'll promise to practice for our next lesson."

"But I can't," Mr. VagenWorgenVurst wailed. "It's too late for that."

"Look, Gemma," said George. "He looks like a balloon in the Thanksgiving Day parade." And sure enough, Mr. VagenWorgenVurst swelled and swelled to the size of Bullwinkle, the helium-filled balloon. He lifted off until he burst through the roof of his little apartment. Gemma and George were no more than specks compared to him.

"Oh, what a terrible thing we did!" Gemma shouted to her brother over the squawks, squeaks, and gusts of wind.

"Yes, we really should've practiced," George agreed. "I'm really afraid he'll burst."

At that very second their bright red, overinflated, furious music teacher exploded with a gigantic "BAM" that hurled Gemma and George into somersaults and out of Mr. VagenWorgenVurst's studio door. Just as in outer space, the incredible speed with which Gemma and George traveled turned into slow motion. As they floated, a large G clef off the side of a piece of music paper floated by and they grabbed on. For a while it was as if the G clef was their sunfish and the whole music school below was a great, dark ocean.

"Are you all right?" Gemma asked her brother. (She had the better manners of the two.) She was also more athletic and therefore had found the slow-motion somersaults easier to take.

"Yes," answered George bravely, though, truth to tell, he was just a bit motion sick. "We're moving so fast that we're in slow motion. We must be traveling at the speed of sound." (George knew many more facts than his sister.)

"George, I feel like we've shrunk," Gemma shouted. They looked down and saw that they were floating across the ceiling of the music store. Below them the basses looked like dark mountains, the trombones like peninsulas, and the tambourines were no more than the whitecaps on the waves of ocean. The dark wooden cabinets that held the flutes and piccolos looked like the dark walls of caves. And all the metal of the cymbals and tambourines appeared like shiny little suns.

"I've never seen musical instruments look so beautiful," said Gemma. "Or so scary." The mouth of the big contrabass was a dragon's gaping smile, and the trumpet's bright horn looked like an endless swirling funnel.

"Look down," whispered George.

There, like the flattest, largest islands on the ocean's floor, lay the heads of the timpani. They were whole lands unto themselves, and Gemma and George could feel their breath taken away by the timpani's great size and their round white beauty.

Within seconds they lost hold of the G clef and found themselves somersaulting toward the timpani. They were scared.

Gemma and George suddenly plummeted straight toward the heads of the timpani, which still seemed many miles away.

"How I wish I had a hang glider or a parachute," George prayed. They were falling very quickly now.

"I *told* Mother I didn't want to take violin this year," Gemma fumed. "And my new denim jumper is going to get filthy. . . . If she could see us now . . ."

But there was no time to finish the thought because the twins were tumbling very fast straight toward the white plastic head of the timpani.

"Watch out!" George called. And they landed with a BOOM. They bounced off the flat head again as if it were a trampoline. They crashed again, KABOOM, and bounced off once more.

"I feel like I'm in the circus," Gemma laughed. She practiced some splits like she'd seen the older girls do in gym.

"I always wanted to be in the Olympics!" George agreed, and he and his sister laughed and bounced off the head of the timpani again and again, playing games and showing off for each other. They almost forgot their strange predicament except that, after one particularly high and hard bounce, they broke right through the plastic head and found themselves once again falling through a dark and unknown space.

"Can you you you you you hear hear hear how it e-e-e-e-echoes in here here here here here?" Gemma said to her brother, whose hair, she noticed, stood straight up.

"The walls are *round round round round round*," George answered. "And metal-l-l-l-l-l-l."

The twins looked fearfully at the copper-colored metal cave into which they had tumbled. Gemma began to bite the inside of her lip even though her mother had often told her not to.

She loved her mother very much and remembered her long thin waist, painted fingernails, three-inch high heels, and flute playing. She wondered if her mother was waiting outside the music store in her Chevy, and she especially wondered what her mother would make of their current trouble. Would she say, "Gemma! Stop making up stories"? Would she say, "You're

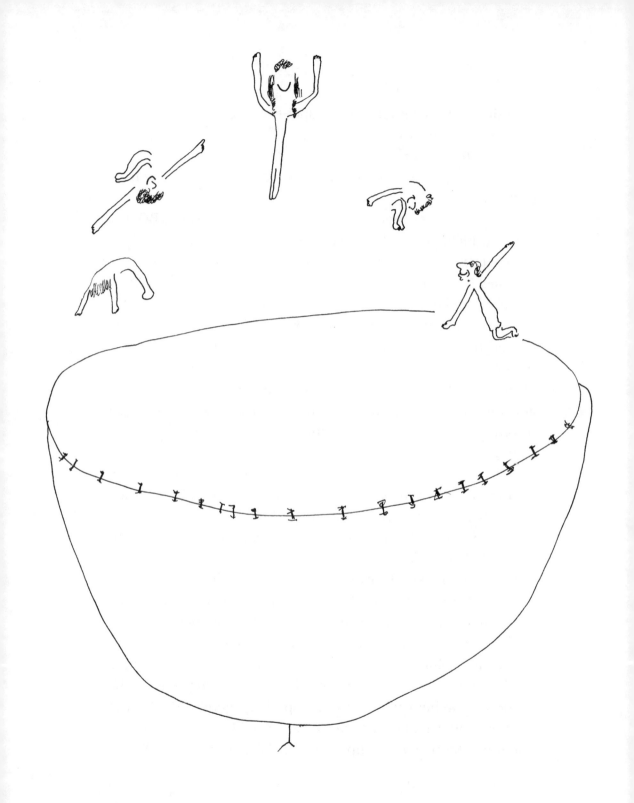

dreaming"? Or would Mother become very stern and say, "See, this is what happens when you don't take your music lessons seriously"?

Gemma also thought about Mr. VagenWorgenVurst, who was probably flattened on the sidewalk somewhere like a balloon stuck by a pin. She pictured Mr. VagenWorgenVurst's studio with all the notes flown off the music paper and the animals flattened against the windows like Halloween decorations. She imagined her mother glancing over at the very expensive timpani with its head torn open and her two children, shrunk to the size of dots, tumbling through it.

"Oh, my," said Gemma. "I certainly hope things can get back to normal."

Just then she and George landed with a *sproing*. They had landed in a multicolored net!

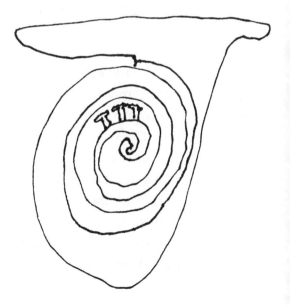

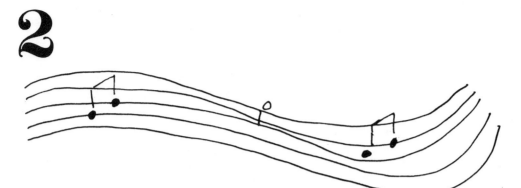

In the Land of
the Timpani

"IT'S AS IF we've just been shot out of a cannon," said George.

There were many nets inside the timpani. The nets hung from nets and looked exactly like those meant to catch you under a trapeze in the circus. They hung at angles below each other. And each layer had little ladders that reached to the nets above. This web of circus nets was a multicolored spectacle.

Gemma heard rumbling and mumbling and low murmuring just like the echo in a well. She looked up and saw hundreds of tiny old men with long beards. They all stood angrily on the nets, hands on hips, and grumbled different complaints at the same time. The whole inside of the timpani was vibrating with cranky, tiny old men.

"It's too dark in here," grumbled one.

"It's not dark enough," said another.

"Will these thunderstorms ever stop?" said still another.

"Can't have enough thunderstorms," said another. None of the old men seemed to be listening to each other, and none of them noticed the twins. They strutted around on their net like ancient gymnasts and grumbled and mumbled. Though none of the old men talked to each other, each one seemed disgruntled, dissatisfied, and disagreeable. Several old men unhappily tried to patch the timpani's head together, but as soon as one had almost finished, a violent wind would shake up the inside of the timpani and he'd fall backwards, rolling down his net.

"I had no idea anyone lived inside the timpani," said George. His voice was a tiny squeak compared to the very low growls of the old men.

"I think I'll go up and say hello to one of them," Gemma shouted. (She was the more sociable of the two, though George was very loyal.)

Gemma tapped an old man on the back. He wore overalls and a faded bow tie. His beard reached down to his knees and his feet were bare. His toes looked like the gnarled roots of an oak tree. His small black eyes were cloudy with distress. He looked very preoccupied as he talked to himself. Gemma tried to shout over his mumbling and rumblings. They were both having trouble balancing on the quaking net.

"Excuse me," she yelled. "How do we get out of here?"

The old man turned around, nearly fell over, and stamped his feet with fury.

"Someone's broken the ceiling, that's why!" he said. "How can you get a night's sleep with the sky torn to shreds? Now the whole place is jiggling!"

"I'm very sorry," Gemma screamed and felt her voice was getting quite hoarse. "I believe we broke it when we fell into your drum here."

"The cause?" The old man shouted disdainfully. His pouting mouth twisted sideways and his eyes bulged. His chubby cheeks went pale. "Why, they've been bombing us for a week now. Shaking up our insides. Dropping things on our heads. Cutting holes in our nets. Scraping the metal sides of our home with scissors. It's enough to create a blizzard in a desert. It's enough to turn a nice old man into a rhino."

Gemma could see clearly that the old man couldn't hear her. His answers had nothing to do with her questions. She looked over at George, who seemed to be calculating a sum in his brain. When George got scientific, he pressed his lips forward in a half kiss and wrinkled his nose.

"I think the inside of the drum is vibrating from the impact of our fall," George said. "It'll stop eventually."

Gemma hoped so, for she was getting a bit seasick. She decided to try to talk to the old man in the overalls once again.

"Do you think this shaking will stop soon?" she shouted.

The old man began to pull at his thick white hair. He knocked himself in the forehead with his own fists.

"They've been planning this for *decades!* For centuries!" the old man shouted. "Why, it's enough to give us laryngitis. It's enough to make us grumble ourselves to death!"

"What are you talking about?" Gemma shouted impatiently just as the inside of the timpani stopped shaking. The old man winced at Gemma's tone, shook out his ears, smiled, and bowed.

"Well, hello," he said in a husky whisper. "Who are you?"

Gemma sighed. "I've been trying to talk to you for the *longest* time," she groaned.

George crawled over and stood beside his sister. "She was trying to talk to you, but you wouldn't listen."

The old man, who looked quite befuddled, shrugged and, once again, shook out his ears.

"I *couldn't* listen," said the old man. "I couldn't hear. *Someone* beat our ceiling until it broke. It shakes like crazy in here, like a veritable earthquake, like the stomach of a hungry grasshopper. Normally, we have five to six hundred thunderstorms a day, and that's status quo. We all grumble and mumble and shake and shimmy. That's our appointed job. But this is extreme."

George bowed his head. He was an exceedingly honest boy.

"I do believe we broke your ceiling, sir," he confessed. "We crashed through like a rocket quite a while ago."

When he heard this, the old man squinted his bushy eyebrows and rubbed his chin with his thumb and forefinger. He muttered to himself. George thought to himself that the old man's very low voice sounded like crunchy peanut butter being spread. Gemma and George looked fearfully at each other.

"Do you crash through people's ceilings often?" asked the old man. He was clearly in a perplexed state.

"Never, before today," George said. He carefully told the old man the events of the afternoon. He began with his terrible music lesson and Mr. VagenWorgenVurst's swelling up like a balloon, the explosion, and the slow-motion travel on the back of musical notes.

The old man listened patiently. Now and then his lips twitched into a silent, angry sneer. Gemma sat quietly on the netting, poking her legs through the holes.

When George finished, the old man looked up fearfully at the gaping hole in the white plastic ceiling. Other old men were scurrying up tall thin rope ladders to try to fix it.

"This isn't the work of mere humans," the old man whispered. When he whispered his voice now sounded like a brush on sand. "Some other, nastier power caused all this to happen. The same nasty, vicious power who has been giving us earth quakes and causing us to vibrate for hours on end."

Gemma shivered. "Who?" she asked.

The old man stamped his foot and growled. The sound echoed for such a long time, George was afraid it wouldn't stop.

"Why, if I was strong enough," the old man shouted, "then I'd have caught the scoundrels by now, hung them upside down by their heads, and plucked each hair as if it was a harp string."

Gemma winced and grabbed her red ponytail in fear.

"I guess that would hurt a great deal," she said timidly.

The old man stalked up to her and stuck his red bulb of a nose right in her face.

"It's not supposed to feel *good,* stupid," he bellowed.

Gemma was offended by the old man's rudeness.

"You're not in a very pleasant mood, are you?" said George, trying to come to his sister's rescue.

"Get *this,*" said the old man. "I grumble. I bellow. I rumble and rasp. It's my *job* to mumble and grunt and complain."

"Yes, me too," said another old man.

"Me too. Me too," said another.

"Me too me too me too," said another.

Now all the old men began once more grumbling and talking to themselves. It sounded like a gentle wave of thunder.

"What's your name?" George asked the old man.

"My name?" shouted the old man. He looked quite annoyed. "Why, it's Mr. BA-BA DADOOM," he answered. "Obviously."

"Yes. Babadadoom," echoed another.

"Babadadoom," echoed another.

"Babadadadadoom doom," echoed many others. The gentle wave of thunder swept through the circus nets inside the timpani again and caused the multicolored web of old acrobats to sway.

George looked up and pulled on Gemma's sleeve. Old men on the teeter-tottery gymnastic ladders had managed to patch up the plastic drumhead.

"How will we ever get out?" George asked his sister.

Gemma angrily tapped the shoulder of Mr. Ba-Ba Dadoom, who was still repeating Doom Bada Doom Bada to himself and swaying around like a drunken sailor.

"How do we get out?" Gemma shouted to him.

"Beats me!" yelled Mr. Ba-Ba Dadoom.

Just then a huge looming shadow began to fall slowly over the plastic ceiling of the timpani's head.

"Why, it looks like a solar eclipse," cried George.

"It looks like a planet falling from the sky," cried Gemma.

"It looks like an oversized mud pie," bellowed Mr. Ba-Ba Dadoom.

"Oh no, oh no," cried all the little old men. "Oh no, oh no, oh no. Here we go again!"

The shadow fell and fell until the whole inside of the timpani darkened as if it was the darkest hour of night and then

BOOM!

with the sharpest crack of thunder, a dark round object broke through the head of the timpani once more and sent all the little old grumbling men flying off their nets in whirling aerial somersaults.

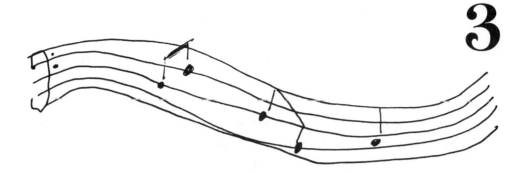

In the Land of the Oboe

"HEELP MEEE," cried Mr. Ba-Ba Dadoom, who, for all his crankiness, sounded quite pitiful.

"I wish I could, but we can't," said George. He and Gemma, holding each other's hands, were now somersaulting too. It was as if the force of the loud explosion had become a ray of sound. It pushed them up, up, up out of the timpani, and then they were somersaulting across an enormous long wooden table.

"I'm getting dizzy," Gemma wailed to her brother.

They were tumbling head over feet toward a round, wide, cavernous mouth made of black wood and ivory.

"I think we're about to fall into another instrument," George observed.

Their tumbles slowed down and they found themselves on a slide. It was as if they were moving on warm ice. It was cool and black, and then they slid straight off into a high pile, a dusty hill.

"We're in sand!" George exclaimed. Sure enough, all around them, for what seemed like miles, was sand.

"Mother's going to be furious when she sees my dress," Gemma sighed. But she began to enjoy the slow-motion waves of the desert sand.

A caravan of men in headdresses and women with veils loped by. They were riding camels. They waved slowly and sang a greeting through their noses. Their language was strange. Eeech-lahah Dombalachazoop! "The music is snaky but beautiful," George said. He and Gemma were lifted to the ornamented saddle on the back of a camel that bumped along. They were offered apricots, dates, and flatbread by the happy travelers, who said nothing, but only sang through their noses. "We must be in the oboe," George calculated.

"I had no idea people lived inside instruments," Gemma said.

"There seem to be whole geographies, countries . . ." George stopped because his camel suddenly knelt, laughed with a high whine, and dropped Gemma and George at an old railroad station that stood out in the middle of the sandy plain.

"A railroad station?" Gemma asked the camel. The camel blinked its two big round almond eyes and yawned. Two tickets fell from the camel's broad mouth.

George grabbed them.

"Look," he said. "It says 'musical train-ing'! Maybe if we find a conductor, we can get out of here!"

Just then a freight train passed, whizzing and squealing loudly. Its engines squeaked and roared. Bums rode on the boxcars and waved to the caravan of Arabic nomads, who smiled, nodded, and went slowly on their way. But suddenly the train screeched to a halt and the cars collided against each other. The nomads sat back down and sighed.

"I've never seen so much confusion going on at the same time," Gemma whispered to her brother.

"You ain't seen nothin a-yet," said a soft, comical sort of voice. "You ain't seen a twenty-seven-thousand-ring circus, have ya?"

Gemma and George turned around and saw a very messy-looking man sliding from foot to foot and falling all over himself. He sang hello in a mellow scat song:

> *I'm the hobo of the oboe and I dance a soft shoe.*
> *My shoes are so soft they be made of cookies and dough.*
> *I can barely barely stand up*
> *I can barely barely sit down.*
> *I never get where I want to go.*

The hobo also seemed very drunk. He laughed and then he cried, told himself a joke, laughed and cried again. When he belched, letters, mosquitoes, and bats escaped from his mouth.

Hobo in
the Oboe

This made him gasp, and when he gasped, his pants fell down. His undershorts were painted with multicolored O's, which smiled, winked, yawned, and sang.

The hobo was trying to sweep up a huge, glowing, vibrating O that seemed glued to the cement floor of the train station. "O O O O H   M E Y E E E," he sighed.

He wasn't having much success and kept ending up standing on his head with the broomstick in his teeth.

"Why are you trying to sweep that up?" asked Gemma (who did not believe in wasting one's time).

"It's just a simple matter of right and wrong," said the hobo (even on his head Gemma could tell his feelings were hurt).

"The O is supposed to be up and down — as you and I are — not flat on its back like an armadillo."

"An armadillo?" George asked. "Armadillos aren't flat on their backs."

"Exactly!" said the hobo. He did a handspring and, belching and swaying, righted himself. "I could tell from the moment I first saw you that you are the heroes sent to save the day. Not that the *day* needs saving, mind you — the *day* seems perfectly all right. It's everything else that's in a muddle. Like this O on the floor which is the door to our picnic."

The hobo explained,

> *"Every year about this time*
> all *of us join together in the*
> *great green field and join in for*
> *a most glorious Harmony Picnic.*
> *Why, children, it makes cake seem dull.*

> *"This year, however, each land*
> *has been having problem after problem*

putting together their float or
ride. No one can get their mechanics
working or their tunes in time or
even in tune. It's shocking.
It's aggravating. Our Harmony
Picnic means everything to us. Without the O door. Without
our yearly parade and feast, there'd
be no music. And without no music there'd be no peace"
. . . now the hobo started to sob.

George was very keen on the idea of being someone's hero, righting wrong. He imagined himself in a uniform with medals and a sword. It was just that, as of yet, he hadn't been able to figure out what was wrong.

"What can we do?" George asked.

"Help me get this O off the ground," said the hobo. "That's a start. It's the opening through which you get in and out of this oboe. Some notorious music haters have flattened it. Now there's no getting free. The trains will stall. The nomads will stand still and my soft shoes will grow hard. There'll be no air or sky or refreshments."

"That's terrible," Gemma agreed.

So the three of them pried, pushed, heaved, and ho-hoed until finally the glowing, shimmering O stood upright and became the same ebony cave through which Gemma and George had tumbled in the first place. The freight train started up again and the nomads once again began their wandering.

"You are two genu-ine heroes," said the hobo. "And I will never forget how you rushed in and carried me out from that burning hotel."

"We didn't do that," said Gemma.

"I know, but it sounds better that way."

"But we wouldn't want you to lie," said George.

The O began to tilt precariously and the hobo tried to hold it up and balance it. He twisted his rubbery body into several strange shapes, making himself laugh and belch all the while.

"You got to make the best out of a terrible situation," he said. "In this land, it's whatever sounds good!"

A force as strong as a magnet kept trying to flatten the O, and the train and hoboes kept being stalled, and all the nomads kept falling into the sand and getting up. The train was barely making it through the tilting O.

"Have you got your train-ing tickets?" gasped the hobo.

"Yes," George announced.

"Then get on, get on — get out of here and find the culprits who are flattening the O and closing us off from the outside. Why, you're the greatest heroes since Ruff 'n' Ready — I know you two can do it."

"Ruff 'n' Ready weren't heroes that I know of," said Gemma.

"I know, I know," said the hobo, but it *sounds* good. Inside here we do a lotta what *sounds* good!" George and Gemma patted their new friend on his raggedy shoulders and watched him slump and slide as he carried the weight of the slipping O on his back. Suddenly a huffing, smoking passenger train pulled up and it had MUSIKAL TRAIN-ING misspelled on its side. A large gray heron in a navy-blue uniform stepped out and wordlessly motioned to the twins with a long white conductor's baton. The hobo motioned to a boxcar full of yawning and sleeping creatures.

"You better get a-bored if you ain't a-bored now," he said. He laughed and hiccupped. But then his grubby face turned quite serious.

"You get those villains," he yelled drunkenly.

"Save our picnic! Save our lands! Save our people!"

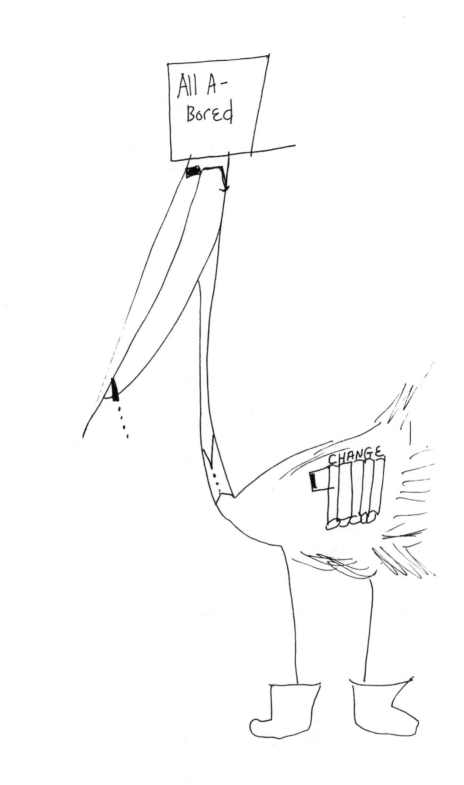

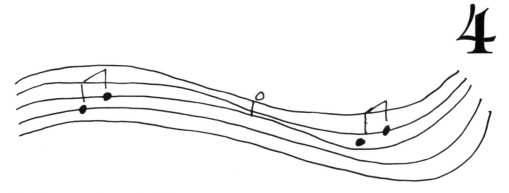

Musikal Train-ing

THE TWINS sat on the train and watched as they tunneled noisily through the ebony funnel of the oboe's mouth. They didn't know where they were going or what villains they were looking for. The other passengers on the train ranged from fireflies to men who resembled chemistry professors, from fat snails to tiny minnows rowing in crab claws, from elderly ladies knitting each other's bonnets to strange-shaped banging bones and many plump, laughing men. As usual, in situations where they were confused or afraid, the twins held hands and began to thumb wrestle.

"This is the Instrumental Alphabetical Spectacular Choo Choo," the conductor called out. And indeed, it was a ride like no other. Once outside the dark tube of the oboe, a whole universe opened up from the windows where Gemma and George sat. It was a universe totally different from the Milky Way (about which George had been quite interested in school). The sky was white as parchment, and there were suns, stars, and moons, drawn out of notes, clefs, and staves. This universe reminded the twins of their music lessons. A violin floated below, and it looked like the peninsula of Italy. Several sizes of timpani rolled by like Saturn and its rings. Flutes made formations like the rays of light around the sun.

"Yes, it was a beautiful world," said the heron, "until the spoilers came."

"What did they do?" asked Gemma.

"Look for yerself," said the conductor, pointing his baton like a wand. "When we reach our first stop."

Then came an announcement:

"All wishing to disembark (not counting dogs who want to keep their bark) will now take heed. We are stopping not at AA nor AB but AC, in fact, ACC. The accordian for polkaing, partying, and promenading."

The train screeched to a halt. The twins looked out at a large German garden filled with multicolored flowers and picnic tables. There was a large lawn for dancing, but it remained empty. Though the train stopped for only a brief moment, Gemma spotted a number of jolly-looking trolls passed out with their heads in their mugs. They snored and wheezed and flopped over onto the ground.

"Used to be the greatest polka dancers in the world," said the heron. "Now they're unconscious, they are. Someone's spiked their beer."

The train squealed and took off again. Shortly Gemma looked outside and saw a row of basset hounds dressed in tuxedos and derbies, holding briefcases and umbrellas. They waved as the train shot by them. The stop said "BASSOON." A lady with a porcine face and granny glasses leaned back to the twins and whispered through her snout.

"Can't pick up the likes of them these days," she said. "They're too sad. Things are sad enough as is!" And sure enough, as the

train passed the bassoon-dwellers by, Gemma and George heard a howling noise that made their eyes burn with tears.

"Arghawghnggrranglpfaws," howled the dogs. It sounded the way a huge lemon would taste.

"What I wouldn't give for the old days when a tail would wag once in a while," said the lady with the porcine face.

Once again the conductor made a loud announcement:

"We're entering the B's yessiree the BA yessirees the BAG yessiree, bring your plaids it's time for a visit in the bagpipes."

The train halted itself inside a plaid world.

"You can take a stretch," the conductor told the twins. "We're changing strings on the engine. Most plaids stretch anyway."

What a fantastic land there was inside the bagpipe! The grass, sky, and trees were all plaid. The sheep and goats were plaid too. The sky was made of cloth and you could tug at it. All the birds, animals, and insects were kilts.

"Nothing seems to be very wrong here," Gemma said hopefully.

But just as she spoke, an army of men in kilts marched forward, and their captain, a man with a plaid mustache, shouted.

"Breathe in!"

The army did as it was told and the whole countryside fell over, sucked in by the breath of the army. It was like a vacuum-cleaner storm. All the tourists as well as the population of the bagpipe slid against the wall of a nearby barn. Their feet just slid flat out.

"Oh, my," Gemma called out. "I'm tumbling again!" She and George were getting quite used to their feet being off the ground.

Just as soon as the crowd landed by the barn, the captain called, "Breathe out!" and the army breathed out, causing the whole countryside to roll back into its original position.

"I don't think I'd like to go on like this all day," said George. He tried to lead his sister back to the train, but the breathing in and out were so strong it was very hard not to be sent tumbling to the left or right in the plaid countryside.

"That was a close call," said the lady with the porcine face when they finally returned to their seats. "Sightseeing is one thing I'd never do in these sort of off-beat times. Not me. Not even if I had an umbrella, which I don't."

Gemma and George watched as the Musikal Train-ing traveled through several other countries inside instruments. Inside each country something was very wrong. The train hummed through tunnels scrawled with graffiti. The graffiti read, "Down With Musick Up With Horribleness." The train whistled over bridges, and signs were hung that said, "NO MORE HARMONY!" The train zoomed to so many places it choo-chooed in rhymes and carried the twins to countries in many different times.

The train ride went on for a time. It was hard to say whether it was a long or short time since everything in this land of music seemed to be measured differently. Strange, too, that the pictures outside the windows became songs. And the conversation within the car of the train became lyrics and sounds. Gemma and George found that they stopped simply talking but were singing to each other. Soon enough all the other creatures began to sing too. Each instrument they passed through was no longer just a country, it was a melody with words and a beat.

The first instrument that became a song was the bass.

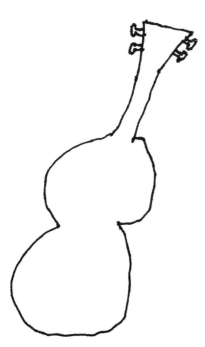

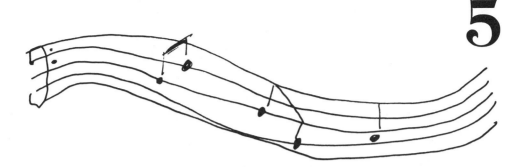

A Longeye View
of Many Lands

IN THE BASS WERE BOPPERS

In the bass there were boppers
who sang bodee oh doh.
There just wasn't anywhere their feets didn't go.
They wore black berets and some real hip shades.
And you know a lot of strolling walking sounds got made.
They had long thin legs and walked so relaxed.
They smiled all the time — that's a fact.
They said —
"Hey!"
to each other,
were the closest of friends
like sisters and brothers.
They sang a kind of scat that
was a language all its own.
Listen to the scat when the scat got goin:

5

Can you say
Bo di oh dee da . . .
Biddly doh day . . .
Shabba shabba do dah . . .
Have a nice day!
Biddly Boodee Doodee . . .
Dap Dap Doh . . .
Gubba Dabba Sciddley Wah . . .
Here we go . . .
Dadda Deeboh Bada . . .
Yabba du doh . . .
Scooby do wah . . .
Don't you know!

The harpsichord became a chorale with large groups of people joining in!

Yes, the harpsichord was like a spa. Tourists got in bathing suits and towels, carrying umbrellas and beachballs.

UP AND DOWN THE HARPSICHORD

Up and down the harpsichord
a travel story got told.
You started out as a baby,
then you grew very very old.
At the top and squeaky high end
everyone sang "tay day,"
then gradually you moved down the scale
and your hair turned gray.
Even plants just started out

as itty-bitty seeds,
but once across the keyboard
became flowers trees or weeds.
Little infant children crawling on their knees
changed to full-grown men and women
by crossing cross the keys.

CHORUS:
Older younger
Older younger
up and down
up and down

If you're six and you
want to be eleven,
jump five steps — — — — that's right.
If you're seven and want to try fifty
climb forty-three steps and what a sight!
Whether you're ninety-six or one,
you stay on the run.
Jump through ages, keys, and ranges! —
What exciting changes!

CHORUS

And sometimes you move so very fast
that a particular age never lasts.
You're six you're forty twelve then nine,
you can be seven ages at the exact same time.
(That's a chord.)

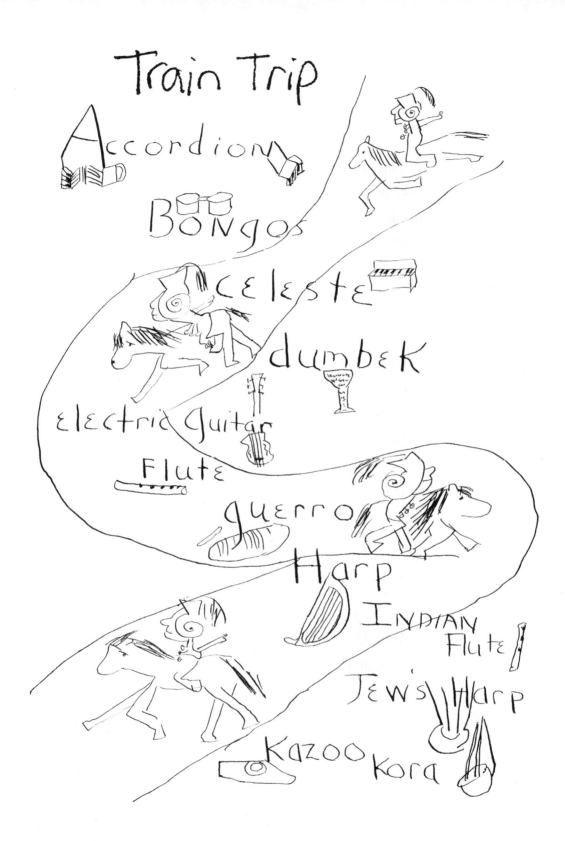

Train Trip

Accordion

Bongos

Celeste

dumbek

electric guitar

Flute

guerro

Harp

INDIAN Flute

Jew's Harp

Kazoo Kora

A white-haired man with spectacles
and skin so very fair
can carry an atlas, encyclopedia,
and a teddy bear.

A little girl in a party dress
with her face covered in cake,
can compute big sums, play excellent drums
and you should hear the jokes she'll make.

CHORUS

Think of all the people
who are many things at once —
The young and old the mean but nice,
the silly, smart, nice, the dunce.

No one ever stays the same,
not in the harpsichord.
It's confusing and lots of work,
but you're never ever bored.

CHORUS

After the bath, picnicking, and exercise in the harpsichord, the tourists on the train began to demand to the conductor (the heron, remember) to find them a snack shop.

"We want to munch," called out the creatures on the train. So imagine their disappointment when they'd traveled all the way to M to be allowed only to *watch* a country that munched and not partake of any snacks themselves.

THE MUNCHERS IN THE MARACAS

In the maracas were some chewing types of people
munching on carrots, fried chicken, and corn.
They had huge teeth, and big Adam's apples,
and munched from night until morn.

CHORUS:
munch munch
munch a bunch of lunch
crunch munch
brunch munch
cha cha in the maracas

They couldn't share their food because they were
too busy munching.
If it wasn't breakfast or dinner, it was lunch or
sometimes brunching.

They could say hello
stuffing zucchinis, apples, and beans.
They crunched and munched so fast,
there was no food left to be seen.

They couldn't say good-bye.
They had eggplants and pies stuck to their teeth.
These folks weren't even fat
because their bones munched underneath.

CHORUS

"All out, all out," shouted the conductor, "for drama, tragedy, tears, and rhapsody! We're going to take a brief visit to the viola. *Sad* though it may be . . ."

There's nothing like a good cry.

Gemma and George watched with tears in their eyes, though they couldn't remember having any reason to be sad.

THE SAD LADIES OF THE VIOLA

Sad ladies in the viola
lay around and wept.
Their bureau was twenty feet tall
where their handkerchiefs were kept.

They sighed, lamented, fainted, cried,
unbraided their long hair.
There was nothing sweet or fun
that could make them laugh or care.

To say hello was very hard.
They could barely lift a hand
to their friends inside the cello,
those very serious men.

The sad, sad ladies of the viola,
all they did was cry.
And if you ever asked them,
they couldn't tell you why.

"We must cheer up!" cried the tourists. "Take us somewhere Tangy Twangy & full of joy."

"Okay," said the conductor. "Here's the guitar," and they screeched to a halt with a jump and a *braang*.

GROOVING IN THE GUITAR

In the electric guitar were electrified men
with bolts of lightning for arms with metal rings.
And when they spoke, lightning bolts came out
and they went zap and boing and zing.
The men couldn't walk, they could only leap
and crackle off each other, lighting up like fireflies.
They whizzed around and bounced off each other.
They were some really excitable guys.
"Wow," they said. "Wow wow wow."
They clapped their hands and shouted "Hooray."
They clapped and stamped and whistled and crackled
even when there wasn't anything to say.
"Wow," they yelled and soared into the air.
"Wow wow," they screamed and crackled in the skies.
"Everything is so terrific," they said,
"and we are some excitable guys."

After seeing so many different kinds of people, Gemma and George thought they'd surely seen everything. They were ready to go home, but they had to stay. They had no choice. They were moving with a force of magical energy. It was as if music itself carried them away. So they made up a song and sang it together. They wanted never to forget this wild time!

THE NEVER-TO-FORGET SONG

How would they remember all this sound?
How would they memorize?
Is there a camera that takes photographs
from right behind the eyes?
How does
a honk a sizzle a giggle a gasp
stay inside the ears?
Where do sounds hide themselves?
What part of us remembers what we hear?

6

Inside the Cymbal
(and Then a Kidnapping)

THE HERON CONDUCTOR strode calmly beside them. He smiled as much as his beak allowed him.

"We're going to crash," he said. "But don't worry — we're supposed to."

Then came a ferocious loud metallic explosion. It echoed on and on and on.

"Cymbal!" the conductor called out. "Everybody out. It's gonna take hours, as usual, to repair the damage."

Several of the strange passengers unpacked tiny mice, baby birds, and snails from their cases to use as earplugs. When Gemma and George stepped off the train, they were in the noisiest place they'd ever been. Every step they took made a loud crash. A vendor holding tin popcorn boxes full of tiny balls and cymbals stood at the large metal door of a building called the NOISE FACTORY and shook his popcorn boxes so they jingled and jangled. He screamed and yelled.

"Stock up on your noise here — get your noise here! Fill up

on your noise for a year! Buy the noisiest noisemakers if you dare come near!"

With their knuckles stuck in their ears, Gemma and George made their way past the vendor and into the door of the Noise Factory. The inside of the factory was a sight to behold and the sounds loud enough to make the twins' fillings ache.

George stopped still and stared at a large shirtless man with bulging muscles covered with tattoos that read "Kaboom," "Smash," and "Bang." The man wore a metallic-colored crew cut and his teeth were all gold. He would've been very mean-looking except that he seemed good-natured and stupid. He lifted up a huge iron hammer and slammed it into any of the objects he could hit that lay in huge piles around him. The piles were filled with TV sets, china, metal boxes, flowerpots, and glass vases. When the man hit, the whole room went KABOOM, SMASH, BANG, and he smiled with satisfaction and heaved a happy, shy little sigh.

Next Gemma and George watched a tall thin woman in a helmet with wheels for feet skate full speed into thin vibrating aluminum walls. Now and then she fell, full force, onto the hard ground with a *BOOM,* laughed happily, and got up again.

Gemma, who was no stranger to making a great deal of noise herself, said,

"This looks like a lot of fun."

But no one seemed to be having as much fun as the assembly lineup of crashy-metallic brothers and sisters who laughed hard as they smashed each other in loud sounds. The first in line stood wearing a metal glove, which she crashed into the metal helmet of the next brother in line. This helmet of the brother smashed into the metal shoulder of the third, and the third's hit the elbows of the fourth, and the fourth popped his fist into the knee

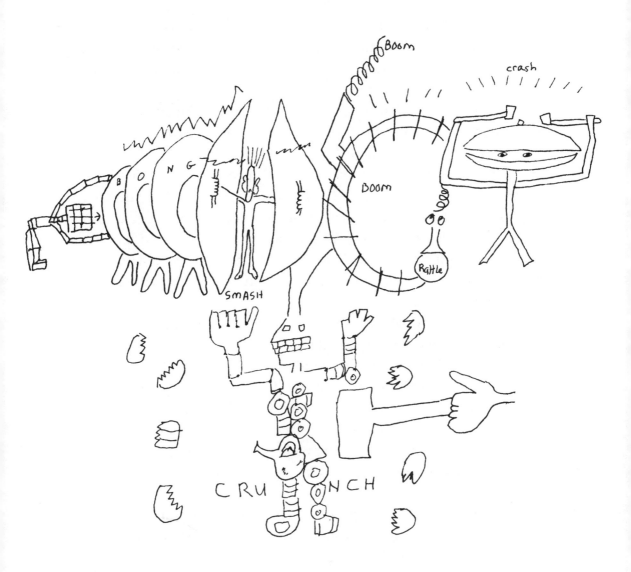

of the fifth. The family crashed and smashed all the way up and down their line and roared with laughter as they did so. No one got hurt since they all seemed to be constructed from tins and metal plates. They rotated on wheels and fell flat onto each other's metal-plated bellies.

"Nothing wrong here," said the heron conductor, who was buying some souvenir noise. "Glad to see someone's having a normal day for a change."

But no sooner had these words escaped his beak than a most peculiar rain began. Felt, velvet, and cotton poured from the roof of the factory. People tried to shriek for help, but huge cotton balls muffled their cries. All the fabulous crashing and bashing became muffled. A high-flying daredevil who dove off a twenty-foot ladder onto clattering pots and pans found himself encased in foam rubber.

"I never thought I'd see the day when it was wrong to be quiet," George said to his sister.

"I did prefer the commotion," Gemma agreed. "I never realized how much fun a cymbal could be."

"And that's just a symbol for all the things you *don't* realize," said the lady with the porcine face, who, as she spoke, slowly transformed into a porcupine with earmuffs and goggles.

"A good sound is like a bite into a watermelon!" cried the porcupine.

"Every instrument has noise to be paid attention to," said the goggled porcupine. "Or you could starve. You listen when your belly gurgles? Wouldn't you?"

"Yes," said George politely (though he thoroughly detested lectures).

"Well," said the porcupine, "every instrument has something to say, and you'd better start listening or soon it will be too late. . . ."

The porcupine stopped midsentence because unbeknownst to George, Gemma had spotted a shadowy figure stealing one of the cymbal-family children. The shadow dropped the crashy child and then disappeared around a corner of the Noise Factory. Remembering the pleas for help from her friend the hobo in the oboe, Gemma set out to follow the culprit, who carried a large roll of gauze and another of cotton batting. But no sooner had Gemma turned the corner than she was snatched up by the collar. A hideous assortment of sharp pinching fingers lifted her off and carried her away. The creature to whom they belonged shrieked the highest, ugliest laugh she'd ever heard — a laugh higher and uglier even than Mother's friend Mrs. Taragreen, who baked sour plum pies and told terrible knock-knock jokes.

George craned his neck and saw his sister disappear around the corner. He was beside himself.

"You're standing beside yourself," scolded the porcupine. "Get a hold of yourself."

But George stood there and, having fallen apart, continued to be beside himself. He was not together. He *tried* to pull himself together, but he was too upset because twins, you see, are closer than all other brothers and sisters. They are often born in precisely the same hour. They grow up with their cribs next to each other and speak to each other in a language they themselves invent. Once they learn to speak English (or Spanish or Finnish or Latvian), they can finish each other's sentences. Yes, twins are so close that they can read each other's minds, know each other's hearts, taste what the other has in his or her mouth, see the exact same pictures the exact same way.

Frozen with fear, George crowded back onto the train, led by the rather pushy porcupine. The cotton, felt, and velvet had been stripped off the Noise Factory by the angry passengers, and the raucous land inside the cymbal had been restored to its crashy and smashy self. But George took no joy in the happy sound because without his twin sister, Gemma, to share it, the world was as lonely as silence.

Miles away Gemma found herself tied to a five-line metal staff, the stems of twisted moaning little notes laced around her wrists. She was traveling in the backseat of a huge limo. The limo was very sharp. Its fenders were made of razor-sharp silver. Its tires were sharp triangles, not the usual circular wheels. Gemma's seat was almost unbearably uncomfortable. The cushions were shaped like little spiked mountains. Gemma peered into the front of the limo. The hideous driver was a man whose hair was slicked back in a sharp, dark, slippery duck's tail haircut. He wore a matador's black hat and off of it hung razors, scissors, nail clippers, files, tiny saws, and sword blades. They jingled every time he shook his head. His overcoat looked like a black tuxedo, the kind Father wore to Masonic dinners, except the shoulders of this coat stuck way out and were embroidered with the mouths of sharks. The man wore many bracelets that had spikes and pins sticking out of them. His fingernails were each filed into perfect points. The spiky man spun his steering wheel, which was also in the shape of a V, and sang a high, squeaky tune with himself. It didn't take Gemma much time to figure out that this man was so out of tune, he couldn't even sing to himself.

"Who's sharp?" he sang.

"I am!" he answered.

"Who's the sharpest?" he asked.

"I am!" he replied.

"Who's his magnificence of sharpness?" he wailed.

"Well, that would have to be me!" he sang.

"Who's the sharpest in the land?" he asked.

"I am! I am!" he cried.

"Who's the Duke of Sharps?" he sang.

"I am! I am!" he replied.

Gemma couldn't help laughing, but her laughter made her arms hurt, they were tied up so tightly onto the staff by the very sad notes. The notes, Gemma noticed, weren't round, they'd been chopped into sharp little triangles. Gemma stopped laughing. She suddenly was afraid.

Meanwhile, the train wound its way through the dark, passing suns, moons, stars, and spirals. George wept through the next three stops. He didn't care if he was a boy; he wept anyway. He didn't see the violins where the timid thin-necked ladies who were full of secrets they couldn't remember lived. He missed the gypsies in the guitar who cried and laughed at the same time as they cursed and told you they loved you. He wasn't even interested in the knights who jousted their own reflections in the circular French horn. George was in a terrible mood. He remembered the time he'd put raspberry jelly in Gemma's shampoo bottle and now he regretted it. He recalled the time she was pressing leaves and flowers in the encyclopedia and he slid an old dead beetle between the pages. He wanted to say he was sorry. He wanted to remind her of the time he greased her bike chain. But he didn't know where his sister was.

"You're not being very practical," said the porcupine, who had gradually changed into a porpoise in a tub. "Crying doesn't do much more than empty out the tear ducts. Even that is a questionable assumption, since one never seems to run out of tears."

"I miss my sister," sobbed George.

"Well, then, *do* something about it. Have a purpose!" said the porpoise, who, though no longer a porcupine, was sounding a little prickly.

George was a proud enough boy to sit up straight, wipe his swollen eyes, and stare the porpoise directly in its beady yellow eyes.

"Why do you keep changing?" George asked.

"That's better!" the porpoise remarked. "I do like conversation so much better than blubbering. I say to my friends the whales all the time, 'Why, if you'd just stop blubbering!'"

"Why do you keep changing?" George repeated.

"Because we're passing through time," the porpoise said. "Everything changes with time. Melodies. Rhythms, harmonies — even your sorry state of affairs."

George looked out the train window and saw that the porpoise was right. They were passing through a city marked ¾ into a town marked ⅝.

"Can't ignore those old time signatures," sighed the porpoise. "They're as inevitable as a flipper turning gray, or your sonar going a little deaf."

"What about Gemma?" George asked.

"What about who?" blinked the porpoise.

"My sister — how do I find her?"

The porpoise shifted in its tub and played with a rubber duck for a while.

"Well, I'd sing for her," said the porpoise. "That's what we do."

This seemed like a foolish idea, but George was willing to try anything. He remembered a song he and Gemma had made up.

It went:

Fat Mr. John Watson fell into a lake
What a loud splash he did make
They had to hang his clothes by the edge of a rake
To dry him off twenty years it did take
With a hum dum diddly dum dum
Chocolate jelly beans and chewing gum.

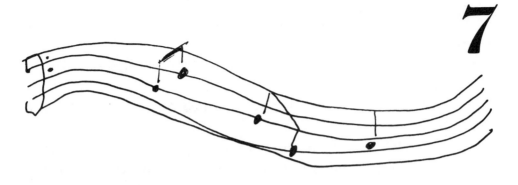

7

TOOFAST

GEORGE WAS beginning to enjoy the melody of his little tune, when the train screamed to a stop and the rest of the passengers, including the porpoise, jumped onto the luggage rack. They shook and whispered, but George stayed where he was. In fact, he could not move for he was stunned by a wild-looking creature who had taken over the whole car. The creature was wearing two pairs of racing roller skates on each foot, knee pads with skateboards attached, and roller skates on both her hands. She had on a bright orange ultramodern crash helmet and her hair stuck straight out in tight long springs from all sides. Her eyes bulged out of their buggy lids and darted constantly from side to side. Her large pink tongue hung from her mouth as if she was constantly out of breath. There was no doubt she was a maniac.

"Issaijack," said the maniac. She spoke so quickly it was hard to understand her.

The porpoise ducked into its tub.

"Good heavens," it said. "That's TOOFAST."

"I know," George whispered. "I couldn't understand a word."

"What I just said," the porpoise answered politely, "is that that's TOOFAST."

"And I said I know," George repeated. "I couldn't understand a thing."

"What I *mean*," the porpoise groaned, "is that the squiggly girl, squirmy thing racing in place covered with wheels is named TOOFAST."

"Oh," said George. "She does speak too fast."

"She says it's a hijack!" screamed one of the men with a clef in his chin. "We better do what she wants."

The maniac named TOOFAST began to roll around the car of the train gesturing so fast and talking at such a clip that she kept sliding onto her backside, flailing her arms in what seemed several hundred directions at once. Her springy hair stuck out as if she'd been plugged into an electrical socket. She seemed a horrible, villainous creature, but George couldn't help laughing at the way she fell forwards over her roller skates and then backwards. She spun several thousand times and then stopped. Her bulging, darting eyes fixed on George.

"Yessir this is a hijack you better believe it is," she said in one breath. "And I'm gonna you betcha take a hostage and then you better believe I'm gonna run away and take the hostage with me yessir I yam and nobody better follow me not anyone whatever you better let me take who I'm gonna take gonna take this here little redheaded-type boy gonna put him in my satchel and take off you better believe it don't anybody try to follow me not even a step I'm too fast.

"I'm too ferocious I'm too terrific I'm on my way gonna take this little red-haired boy yessir don't you try to stop me."

"Someone should've called her TOOMUCH," George said to the porpoise. As he spoke he was sorry he did, for the maniac lifted him up on the toe of her roller-skating right hand and bounced him off her helmet, and he automatically snapped into her orange plastic knapsack, which she must've used for all her kidnappings.

"What're you some strange foreign creature from some other world yeah I think I'll take you you're strange and you have a mean nasty little boy's mouth this'll serve you right," gasped the roller-skating maniac TOOFAST. Then she took off into the countryside, and speeding on her wiry legs and high-powered skates, she flew past the train.

"This girl can really skate," George thought. He couldn't help admiring how fast they zoomed. Every now and then, however, his kidnapper lost control of her balance and began to do what looked like a supersonic-speed tap dance, with her arms going in huge, speedy circles like propellers. When she fell, she fell hard. Sometimes she tripped with a krash. Sometimes she tripped with an *Ak*. When she landed, she fell so hard George shook, trees shivered their leaves, and pigeons went to roost elsewhere. Even when she fell and lay breathing hard, TOO-FAST couldn't lie still. She began rolling and rolling until she gained speed again and could take off.

"Thought I was a squashed tomato that time but you did want to see me pulverized on the side of a rock or mashed like a potato next to a tree trunk well no such luck little weird boy I'm too fast too speedy, too evil I'm TOOFAST TOOGOOD AT BEING ROTTEN!"

George was terrified. He thought he was going to end up like a pea he once saw run over by a steamroller. George knew he wasn't inflatable and if he got flattened, he'd be flattened for good. He had no idea of what was going to become of him. He decided to try to keep singing the song he and Gemma wrote so, if she was anywhere near, she'd hear him. He'd never thought that much about singing before, but he was amazed how the silly nursery song he and Gemma used to sing could still be comforting despite the mad skating of his captor.

Sally Jane ate too much jelly
And she got pain in her belly.
It rumbled like five hundred celli
And made her neigh like the mule named Nelly.
With a hum dum diddy dum dum
Chocolate bananas fruit pops cream and
chewing gum.

All of a sudden TOOFAST screeched to a halt.

"What are you doing are you crazy stop that stop it at once don't you even try that again you stupid little boy creature I'll make tire tracks out of your head do you hear me don't you even do that you stop it or I'll make you into a roller rink."

George stopped singing immediately. TOOFAST sped forward. George shivered with fear inside the bright orange knapsack, wondering what he'd done that was so terrible. He prayed he wasn't going to be flattened out and made into a ramp or circular driveway. He tried to picture himself flattened into concrete or gravel. But luckily he didn't have these ugly thoughts for long because TOOFAST sped her way toward a hideous lopsided castle that was made out of brick, wood, cement, stale gingerbread, concrete, ice, iron, and stuffed vultures. TOOFAST skated up a rickety ramp, and with much spinning and squealing, she lowered herself (and George) over the gate of the castle. George closed his eyes because of the worst terror he'd ever felt.

Once inside the castle, TOOFAST brought George to a dungeon made of broken staves, jagged rocks, flattened notes, and the webs of all sorts of spiders. TOOFAST dropped George, and he closed his eyes again and wished he could be near his sister.

Together Again in the Palace of Evil Do Re Mi's

"GEORGE, OPEN your eyes. It's me!" Gemma had to whisper quite loudly because George's eyes were squeezed so tightly shut, they'd completely disappeared. His whole body was curled up like a shut fist. Gemma had to reach through the bars and unpry her brother from himself.

"George," she whispered, and George opened one brown eye.

Despite the fact that she often told on him and that she cluttered up their play area with her dolls and handbags and that her friends made phoney tea parties with no tea whatsoever and forced him to come, despite all this, George had never been happier to see his twin sister in his whole life. And Gemma, who hated the way he brought home stray puppy dogs and collected boring stamps and performed chemistry experiments on her miniature kitchen stove, had never been happier to see George. They embraced between the bar lines that separated them.

Gemma and George had lived a safe life until now, with their toys, sports, parents, house, inflatable pool, and two dachshunds named Sigmund and Sigfried, so this castle and the dungeon in which they sat helplessly locked away was the most scary house they'd ever seen. Nothing this scary had ever happened before, even in their nightmares, and they hoped that nothing this scary would ever happen again. The dungeon was cold. Drafts and strange sounds whistled through the cracks in the walls. All kinds of bats and spiders hung from the beams. This would have been bad enough for children used to video games in shopping malls, but across a dimly lit narrow hallway there was another cell. And piled in that cell seemed to be *mountains* of tiny sweet and sad-looking dying and dead musical notes: little black heads with crooked and smashed stems for bodies.

"Oh, oh," they squeaked and moaned.

"Is that going to be us?" George shivered.

There was more bad news to come. From an echoing cavern upstairs came the most hideous sound on earth, something that lay in between a siren right up against your ear and your grandmother's evening coughing fit. Imagine someone singing in the most horribly out of tune way you've ever heard. Then add to that someone laughing viciously *because* she is singing so out of tune. Imagine that. Then you'll have some small idea of what Gemma and George heard.

And then silence. A terrifying, mystifying silence. Like the quiet before a thunder clap. Imagine how it feels when your mother isn't speaking to you. How it feels when someone is hiding so close, you can feel their breathing and they're about to pounce. When a wild animal watches you. When a stranger looks at you and is about to speak. When you have to answer truthfully, and all you can do is lie. This is how tense the silence was.

Then Gemma and George heard the sound of very high heels stamping on concrete with a full obese weight. Little squeaks and minuscule shrieks echoed into the dungeon.

"Oh no, oh no," gasped one of the dying notes across the way.

"What is it? What is it?" Gemma asked.

"It's the Queen of Flat Notes," sobbed the broken note. "She doesn't want us to be in tune so she flattens us."

"What a disgusting, rotten place," George said, and he shivered again. "I never thought I'd die being stomped to death by an oversized opera singer."

Indeed, with held breath, the twins could hear Her Diabolical Mistress, Queen of Flat Notes, singing the flamenco she used as she stomped on her helpless victims. (How good it is that the twins *heard* all of this because it must've been *terrible* to see.)

I like my music flat.
I like my notes to go splat.
There's flat notes where I have sat.
And what do you think of that?
Stomp Stomp Stomp
What do you think of that?

I don't like any music pretty.
I don't like words that are witty.
Give me a song that's wrong, flat, and mean
and I'll be a happy villainess queen.
Get what I mean? Ta da, get what I mean? Ta da!

Don't give me symphonies, don't give me harmonies,
no tones called dulcet or sweet.
Anything gentle or slightly sentimental will
get the underside of my feet
(and I'll flatten 'em).

I like my notes on their backs.
I give 'em wallops and whacks.
Then I'll hang 'em upon the racks
to kick 'em sock 'em and give 'em smacks.
Ya da da da da da
Ya da da da da da

"It's certainly clear she likes music even less than we do," George whispered to Gemma.

"She must be responsible for all the trouble that's going on," Gemma said.

"That's going on . . . I would agree with that," said a new voice.

A parrot arrived and was sitting there on the ugly webbed window of the castle. He was beautiful in comparison to the rust and filth. The parrot was green with a blue forehead and bright red and yellow epaulets and had just magically gone and perched there.

"But there was another one," said Gemma, thinking of the sharp man in the limo.

"Another one — I quite agree," said the parrot.

"And another one too," said George, remembering TOOFAST.

"And another one too I quite agree," said the parrot.

"Would you stop repeating us?" Gemma begged the parrot. "It's really very annoying."

"Very annoying I quite agree," said the parrot.

"He can't help it," said George. "He's a parrot. They repeat things."

"No, actually I was repeating," said the parrot, "because as I said, I quite agree with you. You're right. There's the Queen of Flat Notes, the Duke of Sharps, TOOFAST, and others too."

George squinted up his eyes.

"Do I know you?" he asked.

"Last time you saw me I was a porpoise, of corpus."

"And before that?"

"A porcupine."

"And then?"

"A pig girl sort of lady . . . ," the parrot sighed happily. "I seem to be drifting through the letter '*p*' today."

"Why do you keep changing?" asked George.

"As I've told you before, we're traveling through time," said the parrot. "Time doesn't always travel on a railroad track. It goes here and there. We don't just get older or younger. We go sideways, deeper and higher too. Time flies like a parrot, toward bananas, not in straight lines."

George scratched his head, but Gemma's mind was on more practical things.

"How are we ever going to get out of here?" she said. Then she began to cry. This was unusual because George, though no sissy, cried more than Gemma. However, George just cried in little spurts, whereas once Gemma started to cry, there was no stopping her.

"Now, now," George said to his sister. He really had no idea how to comfort her. And the parrot was no help. He was sobbing too.

"Aw hawh hawh, you're so right," he cried.

George remembered a little song his mother sang when either he or Gemma had a nightmare and couldn't go to sleep. He began to sing it . . .

> *The dreams you make when you're awake*
> *are dreams that you can make come true.*
> *Remember how we sang this song*
> *and it will comfort you.*

Gemma gradually stopped sobbing and began to sing along in a sweet, wet little voice . . .

> *The dreams we shared of how we cared*
> *are what we will remember.*
> *Think of sunny summer days when the*
> *chill comes in November.*

Then suddenly the prison bars, made from the lines and bars from the staves, heaved the happiest of sighs and fell down in a swoon.

"We're out!" cried the twins, and they leapt quietly up the crooked dark winding stairs of the castle.

"That was sure lucky," said George.

For once the parrot didn't repeat what George said. Perhaps he didn't think the twins got out by luck.

9

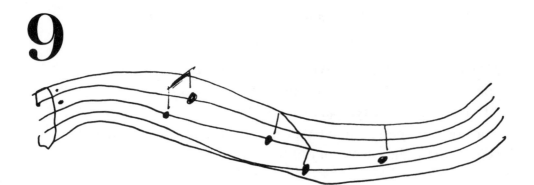

Overhearing a Terrible Plan

THE TWINS climbed to a floor that opened up into a huge ornamental dining room. The large wooden dining table was full of knots, cracks, and holes. Seated on the table was a large and very morose moose whose antlers held flickering candles. This moose-candelabra let out an enormous bra-ay every now and then, sending all the plates, glasses, and silver sliding off the table and crashing into a thousand pieces. No one bothered to clean the mess, but six little notes shackled to each other and serving as slaves reset the table as if nothing had happened. The windows in the dining room were covered with black spiderwebs, and the twins could feel a strong presence of evil, as if something very terrible was going to happen.

Gemma and George hid in a dark corner to be sure they wouldn't be discovered by the moose, the spiders, the slave notes, or the rats who searched through the broken dishes for crumbs. Soon they heard the footsteps of something so large that it sounded as if someone had a garbage truck on each foot. As the giant feet got closer, the moose moved, the candles flickered, the dishes crashed, and the poor slave notes trembled.

And then Gemma and George saw her: the Queen of Flat Notes. She was more hideous than they had imagined. She looked like Mr. Karlofsky the cleaner in a puffy braided black wig. She had a broken big nose and stubble. Her beauty marks were painted on with a felt-tip pen. Her body was so roly-poly fat that it seemed to jiggle in several directions at once. And this was made more awful by the fact that she wore a mini disco dress with fringe and matching crown. And her feet! She had feet that had to be one hundred and eighty-five inches long, if not more! She wore pointed spiky three-foot high heels, and she entered screaming at a note she clenched in her fat, gloved fist.

"I hate you, you sweet little note you," she screamed in her terrible voice. Then she threw the note down and stomped on it with her glittering mammoth foot. The note squealed and was dragged off by one of the slaves.

The queen puffed up.

"And if I hear another sweet sound, I'll flatten it too!" she screamed, and kicked a slave with her heel.

Gemma and George wanted to yell at her to stop but were too afraid. Besides, others were arriving at the dining table. Gemma recognized the sharp man from the car. He strutted like a gangster up onto the dining table and held another poor note next to a scissor he'd pulled from his hair.

"Wazza?" he sneered at the note. "Wazza dis? You ain't sharp enough for dis guy."

Then he cut off a corner of the note until its poor little head was no longer round, but full of sharp angles. The note wailed and wailed as it became sharper.

"What a cruel man," thought George. But he couldn't help admiring his sharp gangster's outfit, with its thick broad shoulders made from the heads of sharks.

The Duke of Sharps kissed the Queen of Flat Notes on her cheek, and his mustache was waxed to such a thin pointy needle that it pricked her.

"Yeow!!" she cried out and stomped one of his patent-leather spats with her pointy, flattening shoe.

"WAZZA?" he shouted.

They were about to begin a noisy argument, when the Queen of Flat Notes changed her mind and summoned her little flattened slave notes.

"Where is supper?" she demanded. "Call the children."

This was a good question not just for the queen but for Gemma and George as well. They had not eaten in what seemed like months or years. There was no measure of time where they were. No clocks, no hourglasses. No thermostats, barometers, or sundials. No Amazonian rain sticks or water drips. No digital watches, church bells, or stopwatches. Normally, Gemma and George would've had a lunchbox loaded with ham and Swiss or peanut butter and jelly, a bag of chips, and an apple plus a brownie for lunch. Now Gemma and George, hearing the word *supper,* each thought about fried chicken or lasagna. French fries or macaroni. A crisp green salad, corn or bright carrots, and pudding or one of Mother's delicious apple pies for dessert. Their minds flashed menus the way some restaurants flash neon signs. Their mouths watered. Their stomachs grumbled dangerously loud.

A group of slave notes tottered in balancing several plates heaped with mounds and mounds of spaghetti lying flattened under thick tomato sauce, a roast beef that had fallen over, a quiche that had gained no height. The Queen of Flat Notes sang a horrible happy tune. A perfect flat dinner. The Duke of Sharps ground his teeth against each other in satisfaction. Suddenly the Queen of Flat Notes' mood darkened.

"Wherever are the children?" she asked the duke.

"Creating pandemonium. Wreaking havoc. Causing a disaster," he replied proudly.

"I don't doubt it," Her Horrible Highness purred equally as proud. "But they must eat to keep up their terrible strength."

The queen sang out a high G note to call the children. It was a note that snuffed out three of the candles on the moose's antlers and caused the ceiling to buckle. The black webs fell off several of the windows. Spiders flew and glass shattered. The moose tried so hard not to bray that he puffed up and trembled.

He feared what would happen if he sent the plates of spaghetti into the queen's lap. The little slave notes ran from one end of the table to the other trying to spot and stop the sliding plates as the moose candelabra wheezed.

Meanwhile, the queen's children entered at different places. First came the roller-skating girl TOOFAST with her orange helmet, springy hair, roller skates, skateboards, and now she had a motorized scooter. She raced up the dining table, ate one full plate of spaghetti in a single gulp, and moved on to a second and third. While she gulped, Gemma and George heard her teeth work like an outboard motor. The next person entered looking as if he was made out of megaphones, loud-speakers, and rock-and-roll amplifiers. He had a big mouth, the biggest mouth they'd ever seen. He crashed over to the dining table, and when he sat down he made so much noise that the entire palace shook at its cracks. There was no doubt that this was TOOLOUD.

"PASSTHESPAGHETTI," he yelled, and the walls shook. The moose coughed, and the plates of spaghetti slid perilously toward the queen's lap. The slave notes recovered them just in time.

Next came a small girl whom no one saw. She just arrived. Every time she spoke, her brother screamed, "WHAAAAT?" And when she moved, her body was so limp that it seemed that her very skin was dozing on her bones. Her hair stood absolutely still, and even when she breathed her mouth stayed closed. She was TOOSOFT. When she tried to fold her hands, they just slid quietly apart.

Next came a child who dove onto the top of the table. He wore many pairs of different pants, striped, dotted, triangled, plaid, stars. Shoes piled on top of sneakers on top of sandals. Twenty-seven different pairs of socks, twelve shirts, and his hair was cut in a crew cut, yet he had a braid. He was a redhead with brown and blond streaks. He began to tie the spaghetti in bows around his braid, play cat's cradle with it, mash it into solid balls, and juggle. He talked, gestured, and danced while he did all of this. He was TOOMUCH.

Finally (or it seemed finally), another boy stood at the table (he refused to sit). He wore one small pair of bathing trunks and nothing else. He cut the end off of one piece of spaghetti, and in a quick unhappy motion, he put it on the tip of his tongue and waited for it to melt. He must've been TOOLITTLE.

Gemma and George thought the whole horrible family was assembled, but then they heard something dragging from the stairway of the basement. The dragging didn't sound like chains, but really more as if someone was pulling a large overstuffed Raggedy Ann doll up the stairs. Gemma and George heard a voice call out so slowly that it seemed to speak syllable by syllable: "A Y Y A M C O M I N." But before the TOO-SLOW child could finish, the Queen of Flat Notes began an important and dangerous meeting with her family.

First she had some complaints about the spaghetti. "It's too sweet!" she shrieked. She flattened several of the pitiful slave notes to make her point, and then the surviving notes rushed away and rushed to her again with spices that might help the situation. The queen put generous helpings of lemon, lime, grapefruit, pickle, sour cherries, sour grapes, vinegar on her spaghetti, tasted it once more, and seemed satisfied.

The Duke of Sharps banged his spiked fist on the table. "Babe," he growled. "Wazza? Wazza this spaghetti ain't sharp enough." First he chopped his meal into thousands of tiny slices while the slaves notes, huffing and panting, brought him the spices that might be sharp enough. The duke sliced cheddar cheese, horseradish, garlic, Limburger cheese, Worcestershire sauce, jalapeño peppers, Kurma curry, and poured them on. He tested the spaghetti and was well pleased.

"You see, my little darlings," the Queen of Flat Notes said to her children. (TOOFAST was now crunching on the china plates themselves while TOOMUCH was bathing in the tomato sauce.) The queen spoke with a full mouth of spaghetti.

"We can't have things smooth and sweet. Not ever. That is why we must make it our solemn vow to destroy all the music of the universe."

"Simple, babe," said the Duke of Sharps.

"Otherwise," the queen went on, "I shall suffer from terrible indigestion of the spirit, have a temper tantrum the like of which no one has ever seen."

"The lady could melt ice," said her husband proudly. "She could sink ships. She could level skyscrapers."

The queen batted her eyes lovingly at the Duke of Sharps. "And you, my dear, could make sushi out of every metropolis in the continent."

The Duke of Sharps sliced his hand into the air, making several flashy karate chops. The heads of poor notes flew in many directions, rolled around, and then rejoined their stems.

"Let's wreck music!" shouted the duke. *Let's wreck MOO-SICK!"*

"Now we all know the plan," the queen whispered. "What we must do . . ." But she was interrupted for a moment by a slow thudding and a held-out voice that said, "I ' M M C O O O O M I N—"

The queen sighed and went on.

"What we must do," she repeated, "is create a big mess. We've begun very well with bashing the heads of timpanis, closing up the holes of the oboes, putting cotton batting on the cymbals, creating allergies in the bagpipes, and causing whatever trouble

we can wherever we go. But we must work even harder now. We must make things messy and noisy and too flat, too sharp, too fast, too much, too little, and —" there came the voice, "I ' M C O M M I N N G" "— too slow that no one will hear each other play; there'll be no musical harmony, no communication, no games, no growing of musical crops. There'll be musical poverty and musical misery and musical famine and musical sickness. And since the people in the instruments won't know whom to blame, they'll blame each other. And then there'll be a musical war and the people who live inside the instruments will fight with each other and grow weaker and weaker until *we* can conquer them all, in one attack. We'll destroy them all — one and all, and then there'll be no more music, no more nicely timed, sweetly harmonious, well-tempered music. Just us — flat, sharp, noisy, crude, rude, and beautiful."

"Sounds hip," said the Duke of Sharps, who was sharpening his fingernail on his pointed teeth. "When do we get all this done by?"

"Tomorrow," seethed the queen. Her face was now red and purple, and her cheeks bulged, and smoke came out her nostrils. "Tomorrow is the day they gather for their Harmony Picnic. It is then that we can smash them with one blow!"

TOOFAST took off for the door. She said, "This is great I can't believe it I want to destroy anything yeah it's great more than I could ever say gonna smash 'em crash 'em kill 'em ruin 'em finish 'em can't wait ready to go here I go ole good TOOFAST can't wait scoobee doo . . ."

"Wait, dear," said the Queen of Flat Notes. "You don't know where you're going yet. And it's tomorrow. Tomorrow. Tomorrow."

Gemma and George now knew the terrible facts, and their

knees shook so badly that the sound of them knocking together threatened to reveal their hiding place. Their teeth chattered and added to the noise. The moose, who still held the flickering candles in the middle of the table, saw them and let out a frightened EAWW that they knew would reveal them. The slave notes were carrying away whatever was left of the dishes. The frightened children hoped they wouldn't be caught. But the moose let out another howl like a foghorn calling to the land. Spiderwebs flew across the room like sails. The slave notes shuddered and glared at Gemma and George. The Queen of Flat Notes, however, seemed not to notice.

"We'll skip the dessert," said the Queen of Flat Notes.

"ARGHWW!" wailed TOOMUCH.

"EYONGAA," howled the moose.

"It was too much anyway," said TOOSOFT, who didn't bother to move her head, neck, or eyes.

"I ' M   C O O O O M M I N G," said the voice of TOOSLOW from the distance.

"Yes, we'll skip the dessert," said the Queen of Flat Notes. "And," she said as she turned and pointed to Gemma and George, "we'll devour those two little cinnamon-haired despicable, spying children instead." She opened her mouth in an angry snarl and it looked exactly like the mouth of a hippopotamus.

Having never been in such a nightmare before, Gemma and George had no idea what to do. Should they run? Should they crawl up the stone wall? Should they take off their shoes and swat the queen? Both had a strong urge to cry. The huge, hideous Her Horribleness was advancing toward them, hippopotamus mouth open, wig bouncing up and down, snarling and squealing.

"SPIES! SPIES! THEY MUST BE EXECUTED. THEY MUST BE TERMINATED! GET THEM. BASH THEM. SMASH THEM. HIT THEM WITH A HARD BEAT. MAKE THEM INTO HAMBURGER MEAT!"

"I wish the parrot was here," Gemma sobbed.

"I wish I was too," agreed the parrot. "Meaning I am."

"You said you could be anything that started with *p*," George said urgently, "so change . . . ! Why can't you become a partridge, no — a piranha — no — a penguin — no — how about a pelican?"

"You got it," said the pelican. "Hop in my mail sack."

Gemma and George dove into the pelican's large pocket of a beak. It was odd inside, like a leathery pancake folded in half.

"This is half like a knapsack and half like a fish pond," said Gemma. As they looked around, the twins saw goldfish and angelfish and blowfish and tiny turtles, seahorses and snails swimming happily in the pelican's mouth.

Though their shoes and socks were wet, Gemma and George breathed a sigh of relief as they crouched down.

"I wish I'd brought my swimsuit," Gemma thought. "Or snorkel gear."

Meanwhile, the Queen of Flat Notes was yelling, "Where did those nasty little spies disappear to? All I see is a pelican. Who ordered a pelican? Why would anyone on earth want a pelican if they didn't need fish?"

"I ' M C O O O O O M I N N G," said a voice that was nearly at the door.

"WAZZA, WAZZA?" said the Duke of Sharps. "Ain't it jus' like TOOSLOW to get here when dinner is ovah!"

"It's amazing he made it on the same day," the Queen of Flat Notes said fondly. (Even villainesses love their children.)

10

How to Rock

"YUK!" the Queen of Flat Notes shrieked. "This pelican is fishy. It smells fishy, looks fishy, and acts fishy. Tie rocks to its claws and throw it out the window. Maybe it will hit those traitorous children on the way down."

Gemma and George gasped from their indoor pond. They heard a large window creak open and felt themselves move forward. They heard the slave notes moan as they heaved rocks up to the windowsill and tied them to the pelican's legs.

"I'm trying to recall what the great escapologist and magician Harry Houdini would do in a situation like this," said the pelican.

Gemma and George felt the pelican lurch as it was shoved out the window. Then they all, the pelican, twins, fish, turtles, and snails, fell straight down. The pelican tried to fly, but the rocks on his feet were too heavy.

"Here we go again," Gemma said to her brother.

"Don't be afraid," said the pelican. "We have several miles to fall, and sometime before we hit bottom one of us will invent a solution!"

They fell past all the floors of the castle and the bridge and the gate. Finally Gemma said,

"Why don't we sing some rock? Maybe it will make the rocks roll."

"What a totally great idea," said the pelican, and then they began to exchange their favorite rock songs, such as "My Rock Your Rock," "The Rock Is Rock," and "Rock Me On My Rocker Rockman."

Sure enough, at the sound of the music, the rock began to shake, whistle, and pop its fingers. So Gemma, George, and the pelican (along with some fish) made a rock band and sang a favorite song together.

> *Once there was a Rock*
> *who lived all alone.*
> *All he did was moan*
> *until he met*
> *the Roll.*
> *Once there was a Roll*
> *round as a bowl*
> *such a lonely soul*
> *until he met*
> *the Rock.*
> *Then this Rock and this Roll*
> *joined together with an "and,"*
> *flew over the land*
> *hand in hand.*
> *Then this Roll and this Rock*
> *like a doughnut and the hole*

hot as fiery coal
became Rock 'n' Roll.

The rock tied to the pelican's foot was overcome with excitement. It shook; it rattled; it rolled. And not a moment too soon, because the landscape beneath was becoming too close and too clear. The rock worked itself loose and shouted yeah! yeah!

yeah! It spun off into the atmosphere looking like a happy moon or planet. Just as they'd all nearly crashed to earth, the pelican began to flap its enormous wings, and they soon regained a sensible flying altitude.

"Well, where to?" asked the pelican. "I've got to drop you somewhere and be on my way. Tomorrow is the big Harmony Picnic and I guess I've got tunafish to make for the Pot Luck."

Hearing mention of the picnic reminded Gemma and George of the danger that lay ahead.

"We've got to get someone to help," Gemma said. "Or we'll all be smashed."

"I think you ought to try to find someone to help," said the pelican, "or we'll all be flattened."

"It's amazing how much creatures repeat themselves here," Gemma said. "You'd think he was still a parrot."

"*You'd* think I was still a parrot," said the pelican. "But I'm a pelican."

"There's a lot of repetition when you're learning!" said George. "As in math, languages."

"There's a lot of repetition in music too!" said the pelican. "It's because things can grow many different ways at once. Up, down, sideways, in layers — very nice. Too bad we're going to be smashed."

"We won't let you," George said sincerely, though he had no idea how he would stop the horrible queen and her family.

"Well, where to?" said the pelican. "Children best not overstay their welcome in a pelican's beak. Some people think that's how you get born. Or is it with a stork? I can't remember. And I doubt you two want to get born all over again! Why you might come back this time as a frog or a crayon or . . ."

"Sally Cavendish," Gemma said spitefully. She couldn't imagine herself born again as Sally Cavendish. Sally wore goggle glasses. She had plastic green and yellow barrettes in her straight, mousey brown hair, and because she ate so much ice-cream cake her legs were as fat as two baby elephants.

The pelican interrupted Gemma's thoughts.

"You've got to try to save the Harmony Picnic," he reminded her.

"You should drop us in an instrument of power and importance," said George, being practical. "Then we can tell whoever lives inside about the danger. They'll help!"

"Who would that be?" asked the pelican. "You'll have to choose. I'm the worst at making decisions."

"Well, is there a president or a good king around?" asked George.

They were now flying over many instruments that looked like bright and shiny islands in an ocean.

"Well, let's see: we have the knights in the French horn," said the pelican, "but truthfully all they do is yell heigh-ho and ride backwards and forwards through the horn. When they're not doing that, they build armor that is too heavy for them even to put on and swords that they can't carry. They're supposed to be the army, but I can't believe they'd be much help."

George and Gemma didn't notice it, and neither did the jabbering pelican, but a dark, nasty, sharp limousine had begun to follow them and was closing the distance behind them.

"Hmm," the pelican went on. "I could recommend the harp, but that's Angel Training school. They never curse, they never lie, they bake meringue pies and sing hymns. They'd never fight for anyone, not even for those who need it."

The chasing limo was now throwing up a cloud of black dust on the horizon. Gemma looked behind them, saw it, and tugged on George's sleeve.

"We better get out of here," she whispered.

"Ah, let's see," the pelican sang on . . . "There's the lute, but everyone there only fights for love. Men fight men for women, women fight women for men. Men and women fight for each other, with each other — ah, love's something for you to look forward to, but they won't help us. . . ."

The front lights of the nasty limo now looked like the hungry eyes of a crocodile. The crocodile looked as if it was about to snap.

"There's the trombone!" the pelican announced. "The governor lives there."

Gemma looked down at the wide brass bowl of the trombone and back at the eyes of the queen and duke's spiky crocodile limo.

"We'll go!" she shouted. "The trombone!"

"But the governor!!" the pelican began.

"We'll go," George repeated.

Just then the pelican caught sight of the limo.

"Whooooo," squealed the pelican. "Yes, you've made a fine choice." Then he dropped the twins while he quickly flew off to make his tunafish for the picnic. The limo screeched to a stop. Its sharp, bristly mouth opened to reveal hundreds of glittering teeth. Luckily, Gemma and George saw no more, for they were already tumbling down the brass bowl of the trombone.

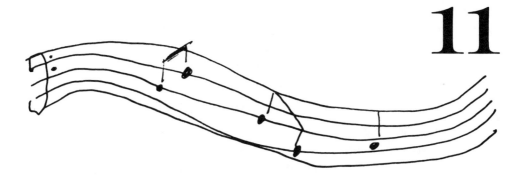

11

Inside the Trombone

THE INSIDE of the trombone looked like a convention hall, with a podium and several chairs at the front and a wide empty floor for dancers or delegates.

A brass band was playing. Banners were being hung from one end of the hall to the other.

As soon as Gemma and George caught their breath, they stood up. And as soon as they stood up, four young men, dressed identically in blue suits with carnations in their lapels, rushed forward. They all were balding and had slick hair parted in the middle, waxed mustaches, and spectacles. They moved and spoke in total unison.

"Hello, how are ya? It's *so* good to see you. What a *pleasure.* What a *treasure.* What a treat! My name is John, John, John, and John.

They stuck out their hands and Gemma and George managed to shake all eight.

These men seemed very busy and important. They carried

with them files and clipboards. They kept looking at their watches. "We're looking for the governor," George said shyly.

"Of course you are, of course you are," said the four men, and then they pinched Gemma's and George's cheeks.

"You're *so* adorable, that's what you are," said John, John, John, and John. "And children too. So much the better."

"The better for what?" asked Gemma, who found the pinching annoying.

"For the photographs!" said John, John, John, and John.

On the word *photographs,* several hundred babies wrapped in multicolored padding were rolled into the center of the convention hall by volunteers. Surprised but unhurt, the babies cooed and smiled.

"No, not yet!" shouted the four men. Then the volunteers dashed in, scooped the babies up, and disappeared.

"Now, what can we do for you?" said the four men once they'd regained their composure.

"We *must* see the governor," Gemma insisted.

"Yes, of course," said the four men. Then, in unison, they combed their hair, checked their mustaches, straightened their ties, looked at their clipboards, and filed their files.

"Next month," they said. "And that's because we like you."

"No! Please," begged George, "we have an emergency."

The four men leaned over. "Everyone has an emergency," they whispered. "The world is an emergency just waiting to happen!"

"But this is a *true* emergency," George insisted.

John, John, John, and John attempted to look at each other, but since each turned his head to the right at the same time, none saw the others.

"We'll have to bring it before the committee, that's what we'll do," said the four men, and they strutted off quickly in a terrible

hurry, looking very concerned as if they had a great many things to do.

George felt hopeful since he'd heard his mother and father speak about each of their different committees, fund-raising, entertainment, charity, flower arranging, elementary school . . . and so on. George knew a committee was a place where you got things done.

But suddenly the big brass band began to blare a loud march. The banners began to wave, balloons fell from the ceiling, and cheers came from all the volunteers who were hidden in the shadows. A spotlight hit the center of the floor and the hundreds of colorful babies got rolled in like slow-motion giggling bowling balls.

"NOOO, NOOO," screamed John, John, John, and John. "Not the babies. Not yet!"

The volunteers scurried forward once again and gathered up the babies. The band resumed playing. The spotlight got brighter. And then there he was. The governor himself.

In fact, he looked a great deal like John, John, John, and John except his suit was made of gray flannel and he wore a derby hat. He was taller, thinner, older, and shaped a great deal like a trombone. His right arm slid out to an enormous length and then slid in again. This made it very easy to wave, which he loved to do, and even easier to shake hands with the crowds of people who'd come from nowhere and lined up. They held posters and banners that said "Governor" or "We love the Gov." The governor reached the center of the floor. John, John, John, and John scurried all around him. They now wore sunglasses so they might look secretive. Then the four men called out, "Where are the babies? We need the babies for a photo opportunity! For hugs, for kisses! For coos! For dimples!" And the babies (by now all napping) were once again rolled at the governor but were so sleepy and heavy that they all landed on him in a dozing heap. The babies, now awake and cranky, began to scream. "No," said John, John, John, and John, "this won't make a good picture." So the governor had to be dug out of the pile of crying babies. He made sure to smile and wave at them as they were hauled away by the clucking volunteers, arms full of quilts, pacifiers, and cookies.

The governor crawled his way to the podium, brushed himself off, and, amid cheers, whistles, and applause, began his speech. Gemma and George were very excited. They'd never been so close to a speech before:

"Ladies, gentlemen," began the governor, "lilies, geraniums, and boytchicals and goitchicals of all ages. Let us remember one thing — let us put our heads together and remember one important thing . . ."

There was a pause.

"What?" the governor asked John, John, John, and John. "I can't remember."

The four men whispered in his ears.

"Oh, yes," the governor coughed. "Jabbajabba."

The audience screamed with approval.

"What's that?" Gemma asked George.

"Shh," said George.

"What do I do now?" the governor asked.

John, John, John, and John whispered again into his ear.

"Oh, yes, my speech. Well, here it is," said the governor.

"Oh, good," said George.

THE GOVERNOR'S SPEECH:

All I would, if I could,
I should and shall have too.
There shall be recorded thus;
right here for you and you.

Therefore shall I if I do I
with a red, green, and blue
I so said always always true I
would for you and you.

"It doesn't make any sense," Gemma said.

"Shh," said George. "It's a political speech. It's not supposed to."

The governor went on:

Well I hum hum.
Yes you um um.
Ought to bee bum,
Diddly doo doo.

> *Jabba Jabba.*
> *Diddle Babba.*
> *Goo Goo Ga Ga.*
> *For you and you.*

"It's baby talk!" said Gemma. And sure enough, all the babies applauded.

The governor went on for the next half hour (or so it seemed) speaking in baby talk. George took a nap. Gemma remembered a rhyme she'd learned in school and recited it to herself:

> *The Emperor paraded through*
> *the streets without a care.*
> *And everyone applauded him*
> *though he was completely bare.*
> *Someone should have told him*
> *but none did dare.*

Finally the governor finished.

> *So therefore I would if I could*
> *(should like to dabble doo).*
> *It's what I want*
> *deep from my gut*
> *for you and you and you.*

Gemma and George chased after him as he made his way through the cheering crowd. He used his sliding right arm to shake hands.

"Thankyew," he said. "Oh, thankyew." Even his words slid together.

George and Gemma made their way up to him and his four

men just as he reached the end of the crowd. He had a Rolls-Royce with trombones on each side waiting.

"Mr. Governor, sir," George called out. "We have an emergency, sir. Please help us."

The governor stopped dead in his tracks, stared at the twins. He leaned back while John, John, John, and John whispered in his ear. Then the governor gave Gemma and George a wide, shining smile. Then he laughed and patted each one on the back. He tried to slide past Gemma and into his car.

"Why are you laughing?" Gemma asked. "We didn't say anything funny. The Queen of Flat Notes and her husband the Duke of Sharps are going to smash your whole world, and we need help to stop them."

The governor's face froze in its grin. He leaned forward and looked at the twins. He began to speak.

"I . . ."

"I wouldn't say 'I,' sir. It's awfully strong," said John, John, John, and John.

"We . . ."

"Don't say 'we,' sir. It's not clear who you're speaking for."

"You . . ."

"No, sir, don't say 'you.' You don't know these children."

"They . . ."

"No, sir . . ."

The governor took in a deep breath.

"Sorry, can't speak now," he said, holding his breath. He threw a fistful of confetti over his own face and went, "Yaay, yaay." Then he jumped into his shiny limo. The limo sped off spiraling down the bell of the horn.

"Well, he wasn't much help," said George.

"He was rude, if you ask me," said Gemma. "A governor should never be too busy to help people, if you ask me."

There was little time for discussion, for just then the crocodile limousine of the Duke of Sharps stuck its snout in the trombone and snapped. It snapped again and swallowed several of the governor's volunteers and some babies.

"We've got to get out of here," said George. He grabbed Gemma's hand and they sneaked right onto the nose of the snapping limo, between its headlight eyes. (George and Gemma played this clever trick because they were determined to do anything they could imagine to save the Harmony Picnic and the sweet people who depended on its good cheer.)

They whizzed in the air on the hood of the enemy's sharp, nasty car. The crocodile car would've pursued the crowd in the trombone, but it became *furious* once it finally discovered the two children curled onto its hood between its eyes. The car kept trying to snap Gemma and George off, the way a horse tries to worry a fly off its nose, and in doing so, shook up the nasty flat family considerably.

"What are you doing?" shrieked the queen to the crocodile limo. "I'll make *sushi* out of you," the Duke of Sharps threatened. "Let's get out of here." The crocodile limo retreated from the trombone just as the brass bell was closing. Therefore, all the people inside the horn were saved.

The car continued to flap and lurch. It was hard for Gemma and George to hold on. Yet it was a little exciting despite being scary.

The twins knew they had to get off very soon. And then they saw the exact place. A tambourine. They jumped from the car and fell down, down, down, and bounced onto the tambourine as if it was a trampoline. Little did they know they had landed right in the middle of a feast — a round table filled with foods from all over.

12

On the Tambourine Trampoline — The Pre-Picnic Party

GEMMA AND GEORGE bounced up and down on the tambourine until they heard several voices say,

"Hey, you're upsetting our dinner!"

They looked around and saw a belly dancer who was eating falafel, a gospel singer who was eating fried chicken, an African dancer who was eating bright orange yams, an Indian Katha dancer eating Parati bread, and a British rock-and-roll singer who was eating a piece of roast beef.

"Welcome to the Bizarre," said the rock-and-roll singer.

"Surely you must mean Bazaar," Gemma said politely.

"Jes, jes," said the belly dancer. "Da Bizarre."

"No, but Bazaar has all *a*'s and one *r*," Gemma insisted, "whereas Bizarre has only one *a*, two *r*'s, and an *e*."

"Yes," said the gospel singer. "We always have a bizarre at dinner. We eat, dance, play games, get to see each other. There are so many of us using the tambourine, it's hard to remember to say hello, and remember, it never hurts to remember to say hello. It's a very bizarre."

Gemma and George were happy to meet such kindly people and especially such kindly people with so much food. The twins didn't need to speak to each other to know they wanted to sample a bit off each of the plates. Just as they were about to ask, the belly dancer kicked all the plates off the tambourine and began to dance.

"Oh, they do like to make a mess here," sighed George.

After the belly dancer danced and the rest of the crowd hollered and hooted, the rock-and-roll singer put on roller skates and began to skate around the edge of the tambourine. The gospel singer began to slap her hands together and wail. The African

man danced like a bird. He was robed and happy and beautiful. The Indian dancer began to stamp, stamp, stamp her feet, balancing on the metal discs that jutted out of the sides of the tambourine.

"How is all this happening?" Gemma asked.

"Well, Mr. VagenWorgenVurst used to say that music can go on in many different times at the same time," George shouted.

The twins sighed with hunger and sad memories of how they'd mistreated their old teacher and betrayed their mother's love and trust. They'd begun to feel very melancholy. Four tears came to their two pairs of eyes, but it was hard to cry when the gospel singer's song was so joyous and the belly dancer's dance told a story of a tiger in the jungle. Gemma vowed to herself that she'd practice fifteen minutes a day for the rest of her life if their adventure could have a happy ending.

"Come, ice-skate," said the rock-and-roll singer. He lifted Gemma and George up and began to skate them around. At first their spirits became much cheerier, but suddenly, with no warning he began to skate very fast.

"I do believe we're being chased," he gasped.

And sure enough, following them around the big tambourine was TOOFAST on her four pairs of roller skates, two skateboards, and motorized scooter. Fortunately, she was going so fast that she skidded right off the tambourine and crashed into the broken dishes.

"Help us!" George and Gemma cried to the tambourine people. "These villains are going to smash your whole world."

But the tambourine people didn't seem to hear. They were busy setting out dessert. The tambourine was now covered with a delicious assortment of cakes, pies, cookies, fudge mocha ripple almond marshmallow ice cream, and granola fruit bars.

"You'd better run!" the belly dancer smiled dreamily. TOO-FAST was digging herself out from under the dinner dishes, but the tambourine people ignored her. They were too interested in the food.

"Follow the silver lily pads and duck inside the flute. There's a soldier in there," advised the African dancer.

Gemma and George took off down a wide road, looking for the silver lily pads. Behind them they heard TOOFAST smash the whole set of dessert dishes.

"Those people are nice enough," Gemma said as they sprinted. "But they don't listen to us. They don't seem to understand how dangerous their situation is."

"Yes," George huffed and puffed. "It's as if they only hear themselves. They can't understand what goes on outside them. They're just like instruments without players!"

The road began to get narrower and narrower and circular. Then it turned silver. And sure enough, there were silver lily pads on top of the round, silver road. The twins saw they were now on the keys to a flute. George and Gemma hopped from one key to another. They hopped twelve times until they reached the dark mouthpiece, and being no longer surprised or afraid, they lowered themselves into the land of the flute.

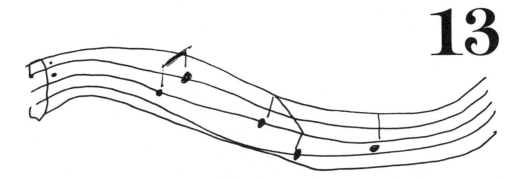

Inside the Flute

GEMMA AND GEORGE had never seen so many birds in their lives. Sparrows, robins, woodpeckers, bluejays, cardinals, and thrushes rested on tall, thin, interwinding branches of the largest trees they'd ever seen. Mynahs, cockatoos, amazons, and macaws hung from the next height of branches. Herons and flamingos graced the nearby ponds, while seagulls and pelicans soared in the air. George looked for their friend the pelican but did not see him among them. The air vibrated with the clicks, caws, chirps, and chitters of birds. Finally an old hoot owl, slouched on the twisted trunk of an old tree, called out to them.

"Oh, good," said George. "Owls are wise. Maybe he can tell us what to do!"

"Hey yooh," called the owl. "Come whohere!"

Gemma and George obeyed.

"Whawhoo what kind of bird dooh yooh think yooh arrrre?" He squinted, rolled his eyes, and sneered with his sharp little beak.

"We're not birds, sir," said George.

"Noo nonsense shoooh," the owl shrieked. "We oh oh oh ohnly have birds here. Now what kind of birds arrrrrre you? A bug eater? A worm watcher? A fish chaser?"

"No, we're really not birds, sir," Gemma sighed.

"Funny joke!" shrieked the owl. "What are you, then?"

"We're humans," George replied.

"Well, that's a laugh and a half with a slap on my calf," said the owl. "That's impossible, you know who who who."

"Why, sir?" Gemma asked.

"Because *birds,* stupid, happen to be brilliant *people* watchers." The owl howled snootily. "We all own oooh oooh binoculars and we have clubs and societies too. We publish books and take photos. Shall I give you a peek through my binoculars?"

"Yes, please!" George said. He was very curious to find out what kind of people these birds watched.

The binoculars were so tiny they barely covered one of George's eyes. The owl showed George where to look. George looked and looked. He saw the trunks of some trees.

"All I see are some trees," said George. He gave the binoculars to his sister.

"Those are people, you stupid bird," said the owl.

"But I'm a person," George insisted.

"Those are trees," Gemma agreed.

"Yooo really know nothing," said the owl. "We've had people-watching societies for years. People-watching clubs, contests, and overnight trips."

"But those are trees," Gemma said.

"What would you know about trees?" hooted the owl. "You're nothing but a bird."

"You're not very wise," said Gemma angrily.

The owl hooted. "What you know about wisdom, a cricket could carry on its back."

"Nor very nice," George added.

"What you know about niceness," the owl huffed, "a grasshopper could balance on one antenna. In fact, I'm being nice as nice can be, I am, considering it's the middle of the night and I'm sound asleep."

"Boy, is he confused," George whispered to Gemma.

"And what you know about confusion," said the owl, "couldn't move a crumb from one side of the table to another."

"You're mad," Gemma said to the owl.

"Personally," the owl replied, "I don't give a hoot."

Just then Gemma and George heard an old-fashioned fife. An old man in a powdered wig and a tattered soldier's uniform limped forward, whistled like a fife, and then fell over flat on his face. "Heigh-ho," he mumbled into the clover.

"A *tree* if ever I saw one," humphed the owl.

The old man began to march lying down. The toes of his battered boots rapped against the ground. Hundreds of birds with binoculars surrounded him and wrote notes on looseleaf pads.

George walked over to him.

"Hello," he said to the ancient soldier.

"Aha, then," said the old man, "you've discovered that I'm a Revolutionary war hero." The old soldier's voice was very muffled, and he continued to lie facedown on the ground, and curiously his feet continued to march. He looked as if he was swimming and doing the flutter kick.

"Yes. Well, someone said you might help," Gemma said. "We're being chased."

"Oh, fun!" said the soldier. "Anyone I know?"

"The Queen of Flat Notes, the Duke of Sharps, and all their terrible children," George answered.

The old soldier rolled onto his back. His wig tilted. He looked vaguely familiar.

"I know a great knock-knock joke," he said. "You start it."

"No," said George. "I know that one. You make me start it, I say knock-knock, you say who's there, and then I don't know what to say."

"It's not funny," said Gemma.

"You mean you won't fall for it?" the old soldier cried. "Then how can I ever defeat you?"

"What do you mean?" asked George.

"Well, watch," said the ancient soldier, still lying on his back. He summoned a seagull. The seagull waddled up.

"What color was George Washington's white horse?" asked the old soldier.

"I don't know . . . ," said the dumb seagull. "Gray?" and then he fell over on his side.

"You see, he fell for it," the old soldier said proudly. "It's a great battle plan."

"How stupid!" said Gemma.

"We can't help it," the old soldier said. He closed his eyes and began to snore a little. It sounded like a trill.

"We in the flute are a bit flighty."

Then the soldier sprouted huge feathery wings and took off like a hawk.

"Nothing appears as it is to be," hooted the owl.

> *Nor is as it was or will be*
> *This shall not turn out as you think it could.*
> *Nothing starts when you think*
> *nor ends when it*
> *ends or how*
> *it should*
> *end. Not even when you think it has.*

Gemma and George were very unhappy. Much seemed to be happening and yet nothing was happening at all. Gemma blinked her eyes and said, "We'll never get any help here."

"This is a confusing place," said a pony who had appeared at the mouth of the flute just when things seemed to be at a standstill. "Don't be so sad. Instruments without people to play them can be a little daffy."

"I'm afraid we'll never get anyone who's sensible enough to help us stop the mean queen," said George.

"And I'm afraid we'll be stomped with the others," Gemma agreed. "We can't see Mother again if we're flattened. We can't play with our friends. I'm afraid we'll end up all squashed and flat, like a picture on the wall."

Then the twins started to cry. One child crying is bad enough, but two is very sad indeed.

"Please don't give up hope," said the pony. "I'll take you to every instrument you want until we find a way to stop this terrible plan. Maybe those with the answer are closer than you think."

Gemma sniffed, "Well, at least you've turned into something reasonable for a change. A pony will be *fun* to ride."

"And what a ride we'll have," said the pony.

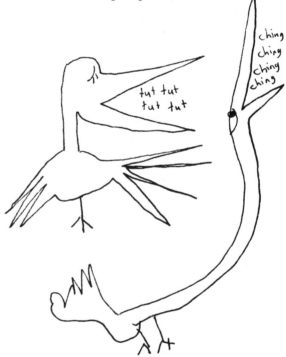

14

The Parade Begins

"Yes, we'll have fun," George decided. "But we won't forget to find help."

They hopped on the pony, took off into the sky, and saw a carnival of shapes and colors beneath them. It seemed that all the people of the musical universe had begun to emerge and were forming into clusters for a parade.

"Look," said the pony. "The march toward the Harmony Picnic is being prepared."

"Oh, can we start at A?" begged George. "I want to see every creature I can!"

"What a sight!" Gemma said when she saw the knobby-kneed oversized Adam's appled chucklers in the Appalachian dulcimers.

"Yee haw!" she cried.

"Don't forget to look for creatures who'll fight the queen," George reminded his sister (he was serious). But she was too busy watching the chucklers, who were too busy yucking and chucking, bending their springy knees and bobbing for apples.

"Look at that!" George called out. He showed his sister the frozen ice people in the Russian balalaika.

"Can you help us?" Gemma called out, but they were stuck in ice like Popsicles.

They galloped to the pineapple, peach, and banana jugglers inside the conga drums who were busily juggling their fruits back and forth among each other. The spirals of the fruit were a sight to see.

"Help us. The Queen of Flat Notes is coming to get us," called the twins.

"Oh, but we can't stop juggling, you know," said the citizens of the conga drum. "If we drop just one banana, the whole theeeng come tumbling down like a fruited avalanche."

Gemma and George tried to implore the tribe who lived inside the Dymbek drum, but they were much too moody to rely on. These people with dark curly hair celebrated, sang, hugged, rejoiced, laughed, and danced — then all of a sudden a fight broke out and men and women pulled at each other's hair, bared their teeth, cursed, punched and kicked, shouted at the top of their lungs, until everyone burst into tears, wept, pulled at their hair, beat their chests, and then hugged, smiled, smooched, and made up again so they could rejoice and celebrate. George and Gemma watched this cycle happen four or five times and then rode on the Epiphone, where one skinny lone man sat all by himself. He was half asleep and weak. "I haven't been used in years," he said. "Wouldn't know how to lift my foot, which foot to put forward first."

They'd already had more than enough of the flute, so they went to the Guerro.

By the time they reached the Guerro, their adventures had begun to rhyme.

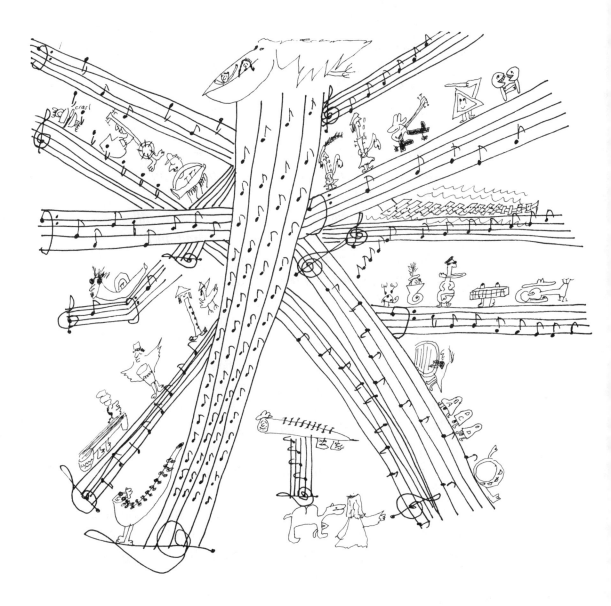

In the Guerro they met insects of a
thousand kinds
with round, oblong bodies, greenish eyes
and tiny minds.
In the Harp they met ladies with corsages
from bouquets
which got caught in the strings whenever they'd
play.
The Indian Sitar held an old, old swami
who twisted himself up like an origami salami.
The Jew's Harp was full of mountain hillbillies
who bounced and twanged and teetered willy-nilly.
The Kazoo had children half human, half duck.
They waddled and they quacked,
then they gurgled and they clucked.
In the Lute the people were very polite.
They wore collars, corsets, and wigs
and tights.
The Moog population was electro-fied
when they got plugged into walls
their words got amplified.
They sounded like rainstorms and teapots
and toasters
humming and bussing and howling like ghosters.

George and Gemma saw that the people inside the instruments were packing picnic boxes, gathering friends and children, and forming a conga line behind Gemma and George on the pony. All the creatures waved and whistled and made it very clear that Gemma and George were to be the honorary heads of the parade line to the Harmony Picnic.

The cheers were loud and joyous.

Despite all their problems, Gemma and George were quite pleased to be leading such a long and colorful parade. The twins, along with the pony, made up a catchy rhyming samba about the parade as they went along and everybody danced.

The people from the Nose Flute
were dervishes and sheiks.
They walked as if they hadn't
uncrossed their legs in weeks.
Hiking and yodeling from folks tall and lean, a
happy group of climbers from the Ocarina.
Inside the Panpipes was a Calliope
on which elves and dwarves rode quite bouncily.
The Quika from Brazil was the Frog Kingdom surely
They ribbeted and croaked
from quite late to early.

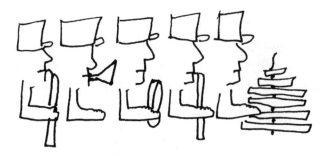

The Ratchet was full of noisy-boned folks
who squeaked like a wheel with
ungreased spokes.
Marches in the Sousaphone frontward to the rear.
Up and down, marching far marching near.
A thunder of marching and calls "Hidey-Ho."
Just so much marching with nowhere to go.
They passed the Timpani and the
deaf old man grumbled.
They climbed off their nets
while they bickered and rumbled.
In the Ukulele was a boatman
afloating on a raft.
You didn't even tell a joke,
but he laughed and laughed and laughed.

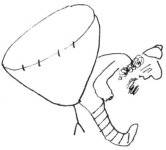

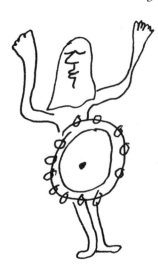

The Vibraphone sprouted plants from buds and
seeds,
bright-colored flowers and long dangling weeds.
They popped on a beat
and they joined in with glee.
A plant is a very contented creature to be.
The Washboard was soggy with drunken bean poles,
The bootleggers swayed and swaggered

while their brew got sold.
The Xylophone people had very small feet.
They tiptoed and looked away from
all those they'd meet.
If someone extended a hand to say hi,
they'd bounce and chortle — they were really that
shy.

The pulsing, happy parade behind Gemma and George seemed as if it were miles and miles long and it stretched out behind them in the shape of a clef.

"This is better than the Macy's Thanksgiving Day Parade!" Gemma called out.

"And we're in the lead," said George.

How quickly their dark spirits cleared up! But, lurking high in a cloud above, a new black murky, mossy space vehicle floated, watching the parade to the picnic move forward. And the ferocious, freaky, fickle, first family chuckled. They had their plans.

They made up their own song:

A NASTY SONG

We'll push their pies in their faces.
Smudge their eyes with erasers.
We'll flatten them to pancakes with
our marvelous machine.
Tell them awful jokes and then *we'll get mean.*
We'll break up their harmonies with hacksaws and chains.
Run over their rhythms with a runaway train.
They'll cry "Mercy mercy." We'll just laugh and curse.
For we shall be the rulers of the music universe.
Yes, the undisputed rulers of the music universe.

15

Captured Once More

SUDDENLY, AS Gemma and George led the parade toward the picnic riding the high-stepping pony, a motorized, sharp metallic arm reached down from the cloud and lifted them from the pony's back. The metallic arm had a metallic claw attached by nuts and bolts. The claw had the sharpest fingernails ever seen, and these fingernails hooked into George's and Gemma's collars and carried them away.

"HEEELLP," they cried.

At first the crowd barely heard. It was not a group known for its listening.

"HEEELLP," the twins cried again.

As they dangled from the metallic arm, they dared to look up.

"Oh, no!" said Gemma. She was frozen with fear. George shut his eyes and tried to imagine that it was all a bad dream. But Gemma and George did not wake up. The ferocious family's new spaceship looked like a large dark lobster out of which eight pairs of mistrustful, smirking eyes peeked. The metallic hand extended as if it were the tin claw of the lobster.

But the scariest sight of all was the billion-pound metal flat foot (modeled after the Queen of Flat Notes' foot, of course) that was attached by rubber bands to the bottom of the ship. All the queen would have to do was lower it and half the nations who lived inside instruments would be flattened. The happy parade was about to end in disaster. The twins were in terrible trouble. Forget the picnic. It wasn't going to be a picnic.

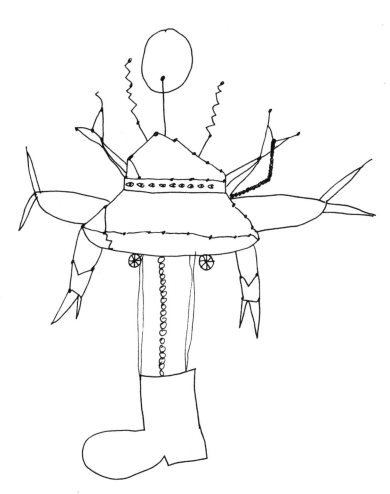

The Queen of Flat Notes and the Duke of Sharps raised Gemma and George into their space lobster shell. Inside, buttons flashed and motors whirred. A TV screen showed the thousands upon thousands of happy people and creatures parading toward their Harmony Picnic. Large groups were gathering on a wide, hilly grassland. The spacecraft loomed above. Five of the queen's six children sat at control boards hitting buttons and raising levers in a too-fast, too-little, too-soft, too-loud, too-much way. Gemma and George finally saw TOOSLOW, who, like a large mass of Jell-O, was taking such a long time to sit in his seat that the others got up and sat down, ate meals, and took naps by the time he got there.

The Queen of Flat Notes stomped on poor squealing notes and tied George and Gemma up to staves by the stems of her squashed victims.

"If you like parades so much," the queen snickered, "if you like picnics so much . . . well, then, we'll make you the main meal."

"Har har har," said the Duke of Sharps. He was sharpening his mustache with pinking shears. Then he sharpened a few poor notes on a stone wheel that gave off sparks.

The queen and duke began to do a tango all around the dark murky lobster-shaped spacecraft. As they danced, they sang a horrible duet that was more off-key than any music Gemma and George had ever played — even on their worst days.

> We will pulverize the people who
> populate the lands
> inside all instruments. They'll be
> as flat as mashed potatoes.

We'll drop a weight upon them
held by a million rubber bands
and they'll squirt and flatten out
like old tomatoes.

"How terrible!" Gemma cried.

The queen and duke danced on. The queen stomped on the duke's alligator boot and he sliced off part of her hair with the shark shoulder on his coat.

There'll be no more music to be heard,
no more songs, not one sweet word.
No more melodies or chants,
just lots of mush like stepped-on ants.

We hate those harmonies and the syncopated beats.
When something sounds awful, that's our treat.
We'll smash the whole world with a big fat heel.
And the worse it ends up, the better we'll feel.
We'll own it all,
every bit.
We'll rule the sour-sounding world
and that's it.

Several slave notes dressed in astronaut outfits tied Gemma and George to the big foot outside the space lobster. The twins hung there many feet above the area where the picnic was gathering. The space lobster lowered down in the sky like a dark thundercloud about to pour out lightning and thunder. All the odd and wonderful people Gemma and George had met — from the hobo in the oboe to the bagpipe army, from the belly dancers and rock and rollers to the gypsies and nomads, and even the governor — were making merry and eating a luscious feast. But when they saw the smoky thick darkness descending, they stopped. They looked up, spied the space lobster, and screamed. They saw Gemma and George hanging from the big fat flat metal foot and tried to help; but even with ten old timpani men standing on each other's shoulders like acrobats they couldn't reach the twins. The Queen of Flat Notes, the Duke of Sharps, and their hideous children stuck their heads from the mouth of the giant space lobster and laughed mean laughs.

"We've got you now!" they screeched. "You're doomed. You're going to be permanently flattened!!!"

The people at the picnic didn't run or yell. They froze. They stood absolutely still. The Queen of Flat Notes began to crank a huge crank, and the metal foot with Gemma and George tied on it lowered toward the frozen crowd.

"Why don't they run?" Gemma asked. "Why doesn't somebody *help?*"

"You can help," said a voice. It was the voice of the pony, but the pony was gone. Now it was a *piano.* "Instruments can't do much without people. Didn't I tell you that?"

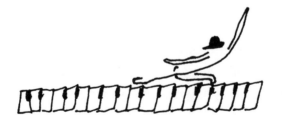

Saving the Day

GEORGE LOOKED at the piano. "How can we help?" he thought. "How can we save ourselves?"

Then George heard something. Gemma had been crying, but now she began to hum. He remembered that Mother always said that when you're afraid of the dark or a bad dream that you should hum so you don't feel so alone. George began to hum Gemma's tune. It was an old lullaby they sang at bedtime. Then as they were being lowered from the crackling, smoke-spitting space lobster, they began to sing.

They were scared, but they kept on singing:

> *Lullaby in the night*
> *ride upon a star.*
> *Make a happy song*
> *wherever you are.*

It really was a very pretty little tune, and the piano couldn't help playing along.

Lullaby don't fuss
what a happy tune.
Think about the stardust
making circles 'round the moon.

"What's that?" cried the Queen of Flat Notes. "I'm beginning to itch! Something's making me itchy!"

"I'm feeling all soft inside," said the Duke of Sharps. "Like someone's crying in my body, but it's not me!"

The teeth of the sharks on his shoulders began to fall out.

"Keep singing," George told Gemma. And then George began to sing harmony (which he did quite well).

Lullaby what a pretty sky.
A peaceful sleep, a secret song.
The willow trees they sway and sigh
and all the stars sing along.

Little by little the old men from the timpani unfroze. The hobo from the oboe began to sing along. The belly dancer hummed. The hillbillies from the Jew's harp added a hypnotic beat. The swami from the Indian sitar twanged. The governor bellowed a long tune.

"I'm itchy. My feet are itchy," cried the Queen of Flat Notes. "Help me!"

But TOOFAST, TOOSLOW, TOOLOUD, TOOSOFT, TOO-MUCH, and TOOLITTLE were sound asleep. They were children, after all, and lullabies put children to sleep.

"I'm going soft," the duke choked, "my knees are wobbling."

Now the boatman from the ukulele, the bagpipe soldiers, the

gypsies, insects, mountain climbers, and hundreds of others joined in. They sang rich chords.

Lullaby! What a night!
To have your grandest dreams.
Oh, the night has much more
magic than it even seems.

The chords lifted up and cleansed the smoke surrounding the villains' space vehicle. The flattened notes, which were tied around George and Gemma, gained strength and untied themselves. The chords like rainbows held the twins and lowered them to the safe grassland.

"I'm going to sneeze!" screamed the Queen of Flat Notes. "I'm so allergic to all this pretty music. It's just killing my sinuses."

Now the whole picnic exploded with melodies, harmonies, and songs. It was a cloudburst and waterfall of beautiful sound. The twins' little song had become powerful. It was a symphony. It could conquer anything.

"AH . . . AH . . . AH . . . AH . . . AH . . . AH . . ."

The Queen of Flat Notes' wobbly husband and nasty children covered their ears.

"CHOOO!!!"

The sneeze was so loud it broke all the machinery.

"AH . . . AH . . . AH . . . AH . . . CHOO!"

The next sneeze tilted the space lobster upside down . . .

"AH . . . AH . . . AH . . . AH . . ."

and the third . . .

"CHOOOO!!!"

sent the Queen of Flat Notes, the duke, and their children

hurtling far into space. All that could be heard was a faint voice saying,

"Those stupid children. I'm allergic to pretty songs. Beauty makes me ill. Bring me my Limburger smelling salts. Oh, no; it's too late! AH-AH-AH CHOO!"

The crowd at the picnic cheered and sang a final jubilant chorus:

> *Lullaby lullaby,*
> *ride upon a star.*
> *Sing your happy song with me*
> *and we can travel very far.*

17

Did He Know?

GEMMA AND GEORGE found themselves standing beside the piano, who had been a woman with a porcine face, a porcupine, a porpoise, a parrot, a pelican, a pony, and now once again a piano.

"You sang that song very well," the piano was saying. And its keys became the teeth of a familiar mouth.

"The notes are very pleased indeedy doody. There's no more beautiful sound than a happy note."

Gemma and George recognized the familiar goatee and beady eyes of their pear-shaped music teacher. Mr. Phineas Vagen-WorgenVurst was standing right there beside them! He was actually grinning. Gemma and George realized they were no longer in the hilly grassland of the Harmony Picnic area. They'd somehow returned to the music room behind the old music store.

"Yessiree," Mr. Phineas VagenWorgenVurst was saying.

"There's no better note to leave on than a good note — a full note — a happy note."

It was clear he hadn't exploded at all. The old music room was in one piece. Even the cobwebs hung there undisturbed. There was no hole in the ceiling; even the window was closed.

Gemma and George stood quite still and looked at each other as if to say, "How did this happen?"

Sometimes twins can even have the same daydreams.

"Yes indeedy, how terrificikidoo. That you would begin your lesson as absolutely the worst musical children in this you-nee-verse and end by playing like angels is nothing short of a miracle. Your horribleness was only exceeded by your sweetness now but how but how but how? *Why, you must've learned a lesson!* Who knows what makes badarific music terrificicooh! But you did it!"

Mother was honking the car horn. Gemma packed up her violin (gently so as not to jar the gypsies who lived inside). George and Gemma didn't say a word. They wondered if they'd dreamed their whole adventure. They looked out the window into the sky to see if they could locate a trail of smoke from the Queen of Flat Notes' space lobster. As they made their way to the front door, they looked at each instrument in the shop. Was the hobo in the oboe? The old men in the timpani? The bebop-per in the bass?

Mr. Phineas VagenWorgenVurst followed them to the door. He seemed to know nothing. He was still "amazed that two such rotten children had turned out so miraculously well." He made no mention of a long journey, a dangerous adventure, or a happy end. And yet, once Gemma and George took their seats in their mother's car, sleepy from so much excitement, they looked back at their old teacher, and he seemed to give a very large and long wink. But perhaps that was just a dream too.

In any case, music was never the same again. Gemma and George became the guardians of all creatures who live inside instruments, and this made the twins practice, play, and sing with joy. Whether anyone really lived in the instruments is hard to say, but you should never take anything for granted in life. You can never be sure.